Savage Light

Janeal Falor

To learn more about this author, please visit:
www.janealfalor.com

Cover by Alisha at Damonza

Other Books By Janeal Falor:
Mine to Tarnish (Mine #.5)
You Are Mine (Mine #1)
Mine to Spell (Mine #2)

Ever Darkening (A Savage Light Companion)

To Rebecca
For being my light in the darkness

Table of Contents

Chapter One

The dark sky in the distance hasn't moved in weeks. Mother and Kaylyn seem too preoccupied with their life-long quest to worry about it, but it keeps tugging at me.

"What do you think of the clouds in the distance?" I ask Jorrin. Not only am I hoping to find someone as curious as me, but it's a good excuse to talk to him.

But it's not, after all. "Mmm," is the only response I get, his hazel eyes focused on something far off.

Does he even realize I'm here?

It doesn't matter. He has a lot to be distracted with. We all do. But soon enough there won't be any distractions left. Once mother and Kaylyn defeat the last evil person alive, there will be nothing left to worry about. Maybe then he'll be interested in settling down. Interested in me.

And I will finally have what I've wanted

for so long.

I stare off in the distance at those clouds, wondering about it. At seventeen, Kaylyn and I are now the oldest unmarried girls. Doubtful marriage has even crossed her mind. Being chosen to bring peace is a good excuse, at least. It means she's too busy saving us all. I left that life when I wasn't needed anymore, and there's an ache in my chest from no longer helping.

An ache I think Jorrin can fix.

"Do you feel that?" he asks.

The ache lessens. Is he finally recognizing something between us? "Feel what?"

"Close by. Darkness. Malryx is chasing a light." He jumps up, making the ache come back with a burn.

Despite the pain, I follow suit, stretching my power up and down the mountain as I do so to feel what he's talking about. My Zophasken, or power, skims across the land, letting me feel what it finds. Plants and animals are all that's immediately close, their neutrality a constant presence. Sparks of light hover around home as they should. I sense other Zophas, fighters of evil, like us doing chores, but as I reach further out something's different. A glow is racing for home, darkness marring the space behind it, trailing after it.

The last darkness left in the world has come to us. It can't bode well. "Which of us do you think he's following? Is it Kaylyn, my best friend? Should we go help?"

2

But Jorrin's already off, going to do what I should have done instead of asking, long legs running up the mountain. Too much time out of the life of fighting has made me slow. I hurry after, moving closer to the spot of light I can feel with my power. It's slowing, but then the darkness is going even slower, letting the distance between them grow.

We're almost to whoever of us is being chased when Jorrin calls out to me, "Marsa, wait!"

It's too late. My heart is already frozen. On the ground before him, mother has collapsed to the ground. Crimson stains the dirt around her.

"Momma!" I rush to her side, rip a piece of cloth from the bottom of my shirt, and press it against her bleeding wound. Little good it does. My hands are already wet with her blood, which makes my own pound within my veins.

"Showna?" Jorrin gently asks. "What happened?"

"Morphrac. Surprise"—she gasps for air —"attack."

"I'm going to carry you back to help. Everything will be fine." But by the sound of his voice, and the blood on me, everything isn't fine.

I move to the side, careful to keep pressure on her wound as he lifts her, and I hurry to keep up. My cloth is beyond soaked when we enter the clearing where the others wait, and he sets her gently on the ground.

Someone thrusts clean bandages into my hands. I pile them on top of the old ones, trying desperately to keep her precious life force where it belongs, but this is beyond me.

"Where's Kaylyn?" And why wasn't she with Mom? Why didn't she prevent this, as is her duty?

"I can feel her coming," someone replies, but my thoughts are so muddled, I don't even know who responded.

But she's right. There is a bright light headed our way, opposite from the direction of the encroaching darkness. She's coming now, but from the red staining the table, it won't be soon enough.

"Momma." The word escapes me, crushing the air from my lungs.

"Shh. It will be fine. Kaylyn... will take care of... things." But she's so pale; the faintness of her voice says things will never be fine.

As if summoned by her name, Kaylyn dashes into the clearing. She hesitates for a moment, just a small, small moment, but inside I'm screaming at her to move. To help. To fix this.

The silent pleading doesn't have to turn to words. She recovers and hurries to the other side of the Mom. Others move out of her way, letting her in. Her skills have to be enough to help. Have to stop the bleeding.

Kaylyn reaches out to check the injuries,

but Mom stops her. "Leave it."

"Momma, no. She can fix you." My heart is being shredded by a thousand knives. This can't be happening. Mom was never supposed to die. She was supposed to live. She was supposed to see her dream fulfilled. There's only one Malryx left: the last remaining evil on the planet is almost vanquished. It's not possible that he should defeat her when the goal is so close.

Kaylyn takes her hand as if none of my thoughts are real. Isn't she going to at least try something? We can't just let my mom die!

"It's my time." Mom's breathing becomes more ragged as she focuses in on Kaylyn. "And yours."

The knives in my chest grow jagged. "Momma."

"Don't talk anymore. Save your strength. I'll find him," Kaylyn says to her.

"Good. I know your final battle will be won." Mom's expression relaxes a little at this. At least Kaylyn can comfort her in her last moments. Assure her that the Malryx are soon to be vanquished. But it's not enough. Not nearly enough.

"Those of you—" Mother coughs, and my lungs twinge on hearing it. Jorrin holds out a waterskin, but she waves it away. "If you haven't… given Kaylyn your power…"

"Hush now," Kaylyn says. "I'll be fine. I'll defeat Morphrac for you as I am. The Aster and Astra said I can do this, so I can."

Mom continues on, driven to her goal even as life pools out of her. "Give Zophasken to Kaylyn," she says between gasps. "She's our best cha…"

Her face goes slack. I gather her to me as if it will somehow help bring her back. "No, Momma! Don't leave me!"

Sobs wrack my body. Pain more fierce than any I've ever felt before attacks my core. The others are talking, discussing. Now isn't the time for it. We have to mourn. Have to! She's gone. From this world. From our home. From my life. It can't be. It just can't. They need to fix her. Kaylyn needs to fix her.

But she's still beneath me, with not even the faintest movement of breath. I press my forehead to hers, squeezing my eyes tight. Any moment now, she'll waken and rise, not even talking about her injury, ignoring it like she always does. Being tough for us. Tough for me. But there's nothing.

She's gone. Really gone.

How can that be?

And the others are still talking like she didn't just stop living right before us. I squeeze her tight, wanting to rail at all of them. Except I can still feel that spot of darkness moving closer. The Malryx never allow time for mourning. Just because this is my mother doesn't make it any different.

The others are right. We have to move on like we always do. I gently close her eyes.

6

There's nothing for the spasms raking through my chest. The best thing I can do now is the thing she wanted. I'll make mom proud. I'll help by doing what I've realized the others are doing. Giving their power to Kaylyn.

I push myself off the ground, unable to take my thoughts from Mom even though I'm leaving her. The sharpness dulls to a numbing ache as I wait for the last of them to finish sharing their power with the one who can defeat evil. When they walk away, leaving Kaylyn alone, I move to her, my steps heavy, and place my hand on hers.

"I can do this," she says.

"I know." She can, and she will. Mom's dream will live on. "My Zophasken is yours."

My power flows through me, down my hand and into her. Its loss leaves me cold, but this chill is nothing compared to the ice inside my soul. Kaylyn needs its warmth and strength now more than ever. The Aster and Astra were right to choose her to defeat the last evil. She's stronger than the rest of us and knows how to use that power. But Morphrac already killed my mother. It won't be an easy fight.

"I can't lose you, too." The words escape me before I realize it.

With most of my Zophasken now gone to her, she wraps me into a hug and whispers into my ear, "Nothing will happen to me, and your mother's death won't be in vain. I'll defeat Morphrac. The world will be rid of Malryx.

Your mother's dream of ridding the planet of all evil will come true."

Tears splash down my face as she lets me go, and Tavo puts his arm on my shoulders. It's true. The evil people that have been around forever are about to be vanquished. Those lying, murderous people.

Something breaks close by, making me jump. Tavo pulls me closer and whispers, "It's going to be okay."

The words feel hollow, though I know they were well meant. Even if Kaylyn defeats Morphrac, it won't bring back Mom.

Outside, Morphrac taunts. "Come out to play, my little Zophaslings. Or did my slaughter of your leader leave you too scared to face me?"

What does a person have to be like to mock someone with a murder? What darkness haunts his soul? This is why Mom's dream needs to be fulfilled. Evil such as this shouldn't taint the world.

"I will do this," Kaylyn says. "Stay in the cave until I get back."

"Vitliruc," Jorrin says.

"Vitliruc, my friend," I say, longing to give her more than just my power and good wishes.

And then she's gone.

With Mom growing cold behind me, it's hard not to worry Kaylyn will end up in the same place. Even if the Aster and Astra are right, even if she is the one to defeat the last Malryx, no one ever said she would live through it.

Today, I've lost one of the two people I'm closest to. I can't lose the other. I want to call Kaylyn back, to tell her it doesn't matter. There's only one evil person left. How much damage can he do?

But Mom is proof enough of how much damage even just one can do. And evil always draws more evil to itself. It grows and morphs, tainting those it touches. It needs to go; only I wish Kaylyn didn't have to deal with it.

The Aster and Astra have chosen her, though. They have guided her though this path. This is what should be. The defeat needs to happen, and she's the one to do it.

The others take care of mother's body, cleaning and preparing her for the ceremony that will likely take place tonight. Attending her funeral never crossed my mind. I stare numbly at their preparations, trying to process it all.

When some time has passed and Kaylyn seems far from the cave, someone is sent to tell the village and the Aster and Astra what has taken place. What will they think of all that's happened? Of Kaylyn's battling for the last time? Of the life that's been claimed?

For myself, it's something I never, ever wanted.

Once done, we sit and wait. And wait. Jorrin sits on one side of me, Tavo on the other. Both stay close, comforting without saying a word. The afternoon passes, and I lay my head on Jorrin's shoulder and drift. Sleep is elusive, but the drifting helps take away some of the pain, worry, and pressure.

Footsteps near. I stretch my Zopahsken, but I have so little left it can only detect the area just outside the cave. It may be Kaylyn. Or it could be Morphrac, come to taunt us about Kaylyn's death.

I jump to my feet, wishing my sword was on me. Why did I stop carrying it around? Right. Because I wasn't needed any longer. It doesn't matter because it's just Kaylyn coming into view, pale and drawn. No serious injuries to be seen. There's already been enough blood for one day.

Unless he got away?

"It's done," she says, easing the last of my fears.

That's it then. The last evil on the planet has been vanquished. Mom's dream came true. Just not before she died.

Chapter Two

The pain grows more numb by the hour, every moment bringing me closer to saying goodbye to Mom for this life. Somehow it's already time to inform Kaylyn and Jorrin what's going on. As I approach, the two are huddled close, Jorrin wrapping a nasty cut on her arm. The tenderness he uses as he works almost makes me wish my arm was bleeding.

Stupid thought to have at a time like this, yet his movements are so soft, his fingers whispering across her skin as he tightens the bandage. I can almost feel it. I *should* have gotten cut instead.

"The ceremony is starting soon." My voice sounds strange, like someone else has taken over.

Jorrin drops his hand from Kaylyn's bandage, but otherwise things are quiet. Are their thoughts wondering where mine are? We shouldn't be having a funeral at a time like this,

11

though there will be a celebration afterward as well. There should only be celebrating on the day when evil was finally vanquished.

I'm not ready to let Mom leave, and going to the ceremony will be just that. It's hard to think we'll be moving onto this new life without her. She's been the driving force behind so much, how will things flourish with her not here? At least with the Malryx gone there's no need for her guidance fighting against them, but I still need it. I glance at Jorrin. Now, more than ever, I need her guidance.

"I thought it would be harder to defeat Morphrac," Kaylyn says, breaking me from my morose thoughts. She sounds like Mom.

"Give yourself some credit," I say. "You've always been the best of us. That's why you were chosen. The Aster and Astra knew you'd be able to do it."

"Maybe, but I guess I expected something more. I've fought tougher opponents."

Why didn't Mom survive then? She trained Kaylyn. She should have been up to the task.

"He was their leader," Jorrin says. "Perhaps he only excelled at leading and not actual fighting?"

He seems to be forgetting Mom too. But maybe there was a reason for the way things happened. Something we'll never understand. I can't imagine anything making my mother's death understandable.

"We're going to be late if we don't leave

now." Can't be late to my own mother's funeral, even if I'd rather skip it.

Jorrin helps Kaylyn stand, and she hurries down the mountain ahead of us. Jorrin and I follow after, at a pace more fitting to the emotions clouding me. The forest is as heavy as my heart, thick with trees, even as we pass the village built on the side of the mountain. I wish Jorrin would talk. Would say something. But then, I'm not saying anything either. It's hard to think of words.

"Do you think Kaylyn's all right?" I ask.

"She's been different. Distant."

"I don't know. Hopefully she just needs time. It's not how any of us wanted to have the Malryx defeated." He looks at me. Really looks at me like I can never remember him doing before. "How are you doing with this?"

My throat threatens to close, but I force the words past my grief. "Angry. If she could have lived past today, the only danger left would have been natural causes."

He puts a hand on my arm; a blanket of comfort softens my ache at his touch. "I'm sorry. She was a good woman."

"The best." I'm embarrassed by how my voice cracks, but he only nods in agreement.

Words no longer seem needed as we continue on. Though his hand is no longer on my arm, the blanket of warmth remains just by being with him, by walking by his side. Does he feel that connection between us?

By the time we reach the village, Kaylyn has slowed enough for us to catch up with her. I wrap my arm around one of hers. Jorrin sticks close to her other side, and together, we stop just outside the group gathered around the pyre. Around my mother.

Despite the silence, many people are here. Probably all who were in hearing distance who could travel. Mother was well loved for everything she strove toward. For everything she did, even when it meant giving up personal things to make it happen. I always wanted to spend more time with her, but her cause was worth the time apart. Sometimes people have to do what they don't want to do for the greater good. I always understood that.

"Showna was an incomparable leader and friend." The Astra's robes flow around her in a swath of black night, the silver twinkling like stars. Mom would have liked that.

The tears start then, hot down my cheeks. Kaylyn hands me her handkerchief, her own eyes glistening, but she's not actually crying. The words make a melodious background Momma would have been bored with, but patiently sat through. She was good at duty. I can't even pretend to focus on what's being said. Kaylyn's handkerchief is soaked before they even light the pyre.

Jorrin wraps his arm around me, which makes me cry harder. It should be comforting, and it is, but my mother should have been here for this. I try to enjoy the comfort as much as I can anyway.

The ceremony seems to take forever before the Aster falls silent. A villager hands the Aster a torch, and it's time. Time to let her go. I can't let my feelings be part of what holds her back. She needs to move on, and I need to let her. The Aster lights the pyre, making my tears come to a sudden, violent stop.

The flames crackle against the stillness of the night until the Aster says, "If any would like to speak of Showna, please take this opportunity to do so."

Everyone looks our way. Though it's not really our way. It's Kaylyn's way. She's the one they all look to now. The one who should be stepping forward to take my mother's place. But she doesn't. She just stands there, gripping the hilt of her sword in the way she does when she's upset.

There's only one way I can think to help her. Besides, this is my mother we're honoring. I have rights to start the memories as much as Kaylyn does, and I know it will help her out. I step forward.

"Mother was unlike the rest of us. She helped pave the way for us to have freedom from the Malryx. More than anyone else, she would have realized what has been accomplished this day and want it celebrated. I only wish she'd lived a long enough to see it."

I move back next to Jorrin and stare up at

15

the stars. The place Mom will soon be. Others speak of her. Of her goodness and kindness. Of her unwavering determination to give us a better world. There's so much good to say about her. That was my mother.

Once everyone who wants to speak has had a chance to, the Aster and Astra toss a handful of something onto the fire that makes it spark. "We release you to the stars."

The flames burn high and bright, carrying Momma's soul to the stars where she now belongs. It doesn't matter what words are said, as long as she numbers among the others who came before us. She'll probably burn brightest of all, eager to light the way at our darkest time. And I am nothing like her.

"Please go and enjoy the festivities," the Aster says, breaking my morbid thoughts. "We have the peace Showna, and many others, always dreamed we'd have from evil people of this world. Let us celebrate that."

The crowd floods away. It feels a little like they're eager to be celebrating instead of remembering Mom, but it's what she would have wanted. What she fought her whole life for. No matter how many times I remind myself it's what she would have wanted, the words never seem any warmer. Never hold any more comfort.

Not everyone leaves to celebrate, though. Those charged with fighting the evil, whether they fought until the end, or their services stopped being needed some time ago, all stay. They wait as the crowd disperses around us. We Zophas are what remains, those of us who knew Mother best. Those whom she led, even when it meant less time for things other mothers in the village did, like making special treats.

Kaylyn is the focus of attention. She would most likely have taken mother's place if warriors were still needed. Even if they're not, she's still the leader they look to, and I'm the daughter that always tagged along.

Kaylyn rubs her thumb across the ball of the hilt of her sword and looks toward the stars.

Mother is there now, shining down on us. I dab my eyes again, hopefully for the last time. At least for tonight. Tears are supposed to be freeing at times like these but always leave me feeling swollen and achy.

The others look to Kaylyn. She appears fit to be my mother's heir as she gives a nod to them, releasing them. They depart, unhurriedly, except for Jorrin. He waits by the fire, staring deep into its flames.

We're supposed to all move on now. Let her life be remembered and her death honored, but not mourned over. It gives room for Jorrin in my life. Tonight will be the night we start building something new. Something we can grow together in. But the needs of my dearest friend come first.

I hold out Kaylyn's now soggy handkerchief. "Thank you."

"Keep it."

It is pretty gross after the night I've put it through. "Just as well. My tears and snot are all over it."

Our laughter feels forced. Hollow. Not what I need to be feeling right now. I glance at Jorrin waiting so patiently. The ache in my chest will be fixed soon. Time and love are supposed to heal heartaches.

"Have you said anything to him yet?" she asks, her voice low enough he can't hear.

"No, but I'm certain he's guessed my feelings by now." How could he not?

"Then perhaps you should get him to the festival, where you can cheer each other up. Showna would have been delighted to welcome a son-in-law to celebrate evil being eliminated."

My face feels fiery. There's no question of that. Too soon for anything like that. "A proposal is unlikely tonight, let alone a wedding."

"You've waited long enough. At least tonight can get you started in the right direction."

The fire doesn't leave but moves to my chest where I've kept all my hopes and dreams. Things Kaylyn knows all too well. Only I no longer know what her hopes and dreams are. There must be someone in her future soon. "Don't fret, sister. We will find you a match soon enough."

She looks to the man I hope to soon make

18

mine, not commenting on my statement. "Go on. I'll be along shortly."

Probably more like in an hour. But if it's what she needs to feel like she can be ready to let Mother go, it's what we'll give her. As long as she doesn't mourn too much and become infested with sadness. "Don't be too long. It's time you learn to dance and play."

The prospect has me wanting to twirl to Jorrin. To let my emotions loose. Since we're still on sacred ground, I let the feeling stay wrapped inside until the festival. Jorrin is somber, still feeling the effects of the ceremony. Or maybe, like me, he's trying to remain solemn while still here. Hopefully the celebrations will loosen him some. I'm ready for dancing and merrymaking. Ready to leave the ache behind. At least for the moment, to try to give Mother what she would have wanted.

"Kaylyn needs some time alone, I think. Let's go have fun, and she can join when she's ready."

His gaze darts to her, but he holds out an elbow for me. He's never done that before: things are already looking brighter.

We walk across the field until we come to a clearing at the bottom of the mountain near the hall where we eat. By the time we reach the gathering, things are already underway. Food out, music playing, couples dancing. The air is potent with their joviality.

"Would you like something to eat?" Jorrin

19

asks.

"Let's dance instead." Food isn't distracting enough. Besides, finally being with him, mixed with wanting to put the day's events behind me, has my feelings bouncing inside me; I'm ready to spin free until I'm so worn forgetfulness overtakes me.

Jorrin leads me to a free spot in the dance clear. We spin and twirl along with the others, the thrill of being thrown into the air and twisted about exactly what my emotions needed. They soar higher than even I do, releasing some of the ache over Mother's death into the cool night air.

After the song ends, Jorrin leads me to a food-laden table. Boys always want food. Maybe I should learn to cook. Not to take over a cook's job, but so I can make Jorrin a special treat once in a while. Let him see what I feel through sweets.

He offers me some sort of pastry, but I don't even know what it is. My thoughts are too jumbled, nervous, and excited for me to pay close enough attention. At least the dancing seems to have helped some. "No, thank you." I wave him away and look out at the dancers.

The song is milder than the last one, not as good at expending my nerves, but still moving. I suppose it doesn't matter since we're sitting this one out anyhow. My feet bounce me up and down, reminding me they want to move, as if I could forget.

Tavo, another Zophas who left shortly after

I did, taps me on the shoulder. "Looks like you could use a dance. May I twirl you around this time?"

Jorrin lingers over the food like he isn't ready to move. As if he's not feeling the beat like my feet are. It's not bad to dance with other boys. Especially when they ask. I'm not hiding my feelings for Jorrin, and it's not uncommon for girls to dance with lots of different boys even when they have a beau or are married.

"That'd be great," I tell Tavo.

He grins and leads me onto the dance floor. Unlike Jorrin, he doesn't just dance with me, but he talks to me, makes me laugh. The sound feels odd, spurting from me on a night like this one, but is a balm to the stinging sorrow.

Tavo's short, curly, blond hair is a perfect contrast to his golden-brown eyes. I'm not sure I ever knew what color his eyes were before, but that's what happens when you dance, I suppose. Though he's not as tall as Jorrin, he's several inches taller than me, so it's easy to twirl beneath his arm.

The song comes to a close, and he grips my waist with both of his hands, keeping me perfectly safe as he tosses me in the air one last time before bringing me back down to him. As the other dancers clap, I hug him. He's warm and soft, and it's so much easier to be comfortable around as a friend than to know how to behave around Jorrin.

"That was just what I needed. Thank you."

And maybe Jorrin will ask me to dance to the next song now that he's had time to eat. "I'm going to go check on Jorrin."

Tavo's suddenly releases his grip on me as he smiles. "I'll take you back."

But I'm already winding my way through the other dancers who are lining up for the next song. Jorrin's right where I left him, next to the food table, gaze turning back toward where Kaylyn probably still is. My own thoughts trail where his gaze is. It's hard not to worry about her. I hope she's handling everything all right and that she joins us soon. It will be so much easier for her to process if she gives into the celebration of everything they've done, everything Mom did. That's why we're having these festivities after all.

I move close to Jorrin's side, Tavo's back already trailing away from us. I wonder who he'll find to dance with next. Whoever it is, I'm sure she'll appreciate what a great dancer he is. If only Jorrin would ask me. Except he starts to grab for a cake as a new song starts. We can eat later. Even our leaders, the Aster and Astra, chosen to help us before I was even born, are dancing with others now. They're almost what I imagine having a grandmother and grandfather would be like. And setting such a good example by enjoying the festivities.

"Will you dance with me, Jorrin?"

"Of course."

He puts my hand on his elbow and leads me

back to the clearing. My feet are ready to move before we reach an empty spot. Once we do, there's no holding back. Our hands press together, arms around each other, feet perfectly in rhythm. We move to the music, flying through the air, twirling, moving together. This is what I've always wanted. This is what I've been waiting for.

The beat thrums through me as Jorrin throws me in the air, catches me, and whirls me away from him then back toward him. My breath is fast. Shallow. Heart pumping like mad. I let the pulse jumping in me radiate through my smile. He smiles back.

Everything is light and free. The music crescendos and ends with a smashing beat, dancers cheering. I collapse against Jorrin's chest with a laugh.

"That was perfect," I gasp out. "You're marvelous. Why haven't we danced before tonight?"

He smiles, shrugs, and looks around. "I don't know. Guess the opportunity never came up."

That's true. We never had much of a chance for dancing when fighting Malryx. But I haven't done much fighting for a long time, and he has done less the last year or so. Why haven't we found ourselves together at a dance before this? I shake off the thought. We're here now. That's what matters.

Jorrin takes my hand, causing a flutter of

excitement in my chest. He pulls me toward the edge of the crowd, and my excitement deflates some until I see where he's headed. Straight toward Kaylyn, who's looking solemn, but is at least here.

I curl toward Jorrin as we walk, unable to stop the laughter from bubbling up within me.

"Thank you," I tell Jorrin as we reach her.

"My pleasure." His words make the fluttering quicken. "What about you, Kaylyn? Would you like to dance?"

The fluttering sputters, and I try to force it back to its merriment. We've been having a good time together, but Kaylyn is our friend. From the drawn set of her mouth, she needs something happy to offset her thoughts. That's the great thing about Jorrin—he's always better at noticing these things than I am. Perhaps the more time I spend with him, the more his goodness will rub off on me.

But Kaylyn doesn't look as if she feels the same about the idea. She purses her lips as she eyes those waiting to dance. "I don't know how to dance."

"I can teach you. It's easy."

"He really is great," I add, despite the strange feeling of reluctance pouting inside. "I'm sure he can help you."

The music starts, and behind me, the dancers begin, but still Kaylyn hesitates. "Why don't you dance with Marsa again? Or another girl? I'm sure they'd be pleased to have you."

"Of course. Marsa?"

The fluttering is back without any hesitance. I grab his hand—when did I let go?—and we're off again. The beat moves through me as it did before, the music just as loud, the dancing just as engaging... but something is off. That happy bounce won't return to my step, even though Jorrin's hands are on my back, arm, shoulder, and my own hand as we twirl about. Touching me like I've always dreamed of. In a way that, only a short while ago, made me excited for the new path our lives are about to take. But now the exuberance is gone. No matter how much I try to let the atmosphere draw me in, there's no way to completely forget.

Kaylyn is upset. Momma is gone. And how did Jorrin and I stop holding hands without my realizing it?

Chapter Three

The week moves in a sort of stuck way. Things try to be like they were before my mom was gone and the Malryx were defeated, but of course they can't be. And I don't want them to. Other than the dance, things can't move forward, either. There's something there holding everything back from taking the next step. It's keeping Jorrin and me apart and keeping Kaylyn from finding her place in life now that our fighting skills are no longer needed.

Whatever it is, I try to spend as much time as I can with them both, to let them know I'm ready to move on with them when they are. Even if it takes a while. I can continue with my duties, helping in the infirmary and the gardens, until they're ready. Even if it's hard. What's harder is not thinking about how much I miss my mom. How much I long to listen to her tell one of her stories just once more.

This morning, the garden is quiet. Too

quiet. The weeds are few enough that I'm almost done with them even though I've only been here a few minutes. The herbs I planted are thriving, twinning toward the light, just like they should.

The thought makes me look in the distance. The dark clouds can't be seen from down here, but when I was at the top of the mountain yesterday, they were still there, and just maybe, a little bigger. I stand on my tiptoes to see if that will help me spot them from here.

"I think I need help," a male voice says behind me.

I turn to find Felix clutching his head, blood oozing out between his fingers. I hurry over to him, trying to keep my face from showing panic at so much blood. It's a head wound. Bleeding is just what they do. "Let's get you to the nurse."

I wrap an arm around him and support him, just in case he faints. His weight is easy to help hold up, though greater than my own. Even though I don't train anymore, I still exercise regularly. It doesn't take us long to hobble to the infirmary. Its central location is easy to get to from anywhere. The nurse isn't in sight, though. I guide him to a nearby sick bed, and help him lay down.

"Brilona," I call out.

The nurse scuttles out from the hall and gasps. "My, my, Felix, what have you gotten into this time?" She doesn't let him reply. Instead, she tsks and gets to work inspecting the wound. She switches his hand for a cloth, only it's soaked in moments. "Lands."

"What is it?" I bend my knees slightly even, though being ready to maneuver won't help. Too many years of training for battle when the adrenaline hits make it impossible to do otherwise.

"Fetch Kaylyn for me, will you? She'll have a better handling on this one than I do," Brilona says.

"Course. I'll be right back, Felix."

"I'll be here," he calls out as I hurry from the building.

It's probably not as bad as Brilona thinks, but she doesn't deal with wounds like this often. There's a need to hurry but not a frantic urgency behind finding Kaylyn. She's been all over the town this week, trying her hand at many different tasks, she, the Aster, and Astra hoping she finds a place to settle into. I don't think such a place is going to be as quick to find as any of them hope.

My transition was hard, but I had time to adjust as my duties as a Zophas slowly ended. She doesn't have that luxury, and today, she's stuck in the barn. Not that it's a bad place to be, but it certainly isn't one I picture Kaylyn in. Of course, I can't picture Kaylyn doing anything other than fighting.

When I reach the barn, I find Kaylyn in the corral sitting on a stool next to a cow. Bet she's loving that. Maybe it's a good thing Felix needs looking at.

"Kaylyn, you're needed in the infirmary," I call out as quickly as I can.

Her head pops up faster than she draws her sword against a Malryx. She says something to the woman in charge of the farmyard, who gives a chuckle. They exchange a few more words before Kaylyn hurries over, dodging the cows like she'll have to go back to milking them if she gets too close.

"That was good timing. Is someone really hurt?" Her eyes are bright as we hurry toward the infirmary, but I can forgive her excitement. It's that adrenaline rush, the power of what we know and do, coursing through her.

"Yup."

"Is it serious?"

"I don't think so. Brilona was nervous about all the blood, so she sent me for you. It's a head wound. You know how those bleed."

"Did we miss a Malryx?" Something sounding a little like excitement coats her words. Almost makes me miss the thrill of a good fight.

"No. It's Felix."

"Oh." Her shoulders slump. I want to reach out and comfort her, but she continues talking as if trying to hurry past what is no longer. "What did he do this time?"

"I didn't get the chance to ask. It's certain to be something entertaining, though."

We head a small ways up the mountain on

the stairs to the infirmary. Kaylyn enters, and I follow. Felix is right where I left him—on a bed, holding a rag to his head, but Brilona isn't. Her frantic movements are focused on getting more rags. "Praise the night sky. He just keeps bleeding."

A little overly dramatic. It's not that much blood. Once, when we were out hunting for Malryx, he slipped crossing a stream and landed on a stick. There was more blood then than I've ever seen, and it took him a month to recuperate from the injury.

"Hi, Felix," Kaylyn says, her voice as calm as it always is when dealing with the wounded.

I hurry to the back room to heat some water while she gets an assessment on what needs to be done. We've seen this before. Probably could have even treated it myself, but she always had more of a knack for it than I did.

I move back and forth between taking out fresh supplies and cleaning things up. Kaylyn has Felix so rapt, he doesn't even seem to notice me moving about. It's easy work, though. One I did many of times on the road. At least here there's plenty of fresh, clean supplies. By the time he's fixed up and sent on his way, I'm already done putting everything away. Brilona shows us out, claiming we need dinner while she makes notes on what Kaylyn taught her.

"Thanks for fetching her for me," Brilona tells me as I head out to follow Kaylyn for some much needed food.

"Always happy to help." I give her a big smile. "Don't stay writing notes so long you forget to eat."

"I would never."

I laugh as I pass through the doorway, making a mental note to bring her something later if she doesn't show up for dinner. Kaylyn is waiting for me a few yards down the path. Now that no one's health is in danger, she should be a little more upbeat, or at least more at ease. But she trails along my side, feet dragging instead of her usual precise steps. Why ever for? Doesn't she realize what a good job she did?

Maybe not. Maybe someone hasn't thought to tell her this is where she should be. If she can't fight, she should be doing the thing she's good at that's closest to what she did before. It's why I work mostly in the herb gardens now. Hoping to help her understand that, I quietly say, "Perhaps you could work in the infirmary. Be a healer?"

"Maybe.

Well, that didn't sound convincing at all. "Do you want to talk about it?"

She shrugs. "Not now. Sorry, I'm still trying to sort my thoughts out."

"Don't worry about it." But I'll worry about it. Never before have I not known what she was thinking. We used to have almost the same thoughts. And when we didn't, we always talked things out. I suppose this will return as we spend more time together.

Time. I can give her that. I can be patient.

And while I'm waiting, there's time to heal from losing Mom. Time to fill the ache in my soul. At least everyone says time fixes things like this. Right now, I don't see how it could, but it must happen. My mother didn't ever seem to have a hole from losing my father to the fight when I was little.

Besides, I've got Jorrin. Things are going to happen with him soon. I just know it. It should help fill the ache inside me. Just thinking of him sparks a light in me. I want to skip to dinner, knowing he'll be there.

The dining hall is within view. Hopefully, he's already there waiting for us. Or maybe he should come in a few minutes after us and then be able to see where we are and join us. Ideally he'd be with us already, but he's working to find good building lumber today. It's fine, though. I shouldn't push things so hard. It's only that, well...I'm tired of waiting. I'm ready, but I told myself I can be patient, and I can. Even if it's hard. Why am I even worrying about this so much?

"What's going on down there?" Kaylyn's voice startles me from my thoughts.

Guilt tugs at me since I've been thinking of Jorrin instead of talking with her. But then, if she was in the mood to talk, she would have said something. Right? I don't know. When did things become so complicated?

32

I look down toward the riverside where she's pointing. A crowd has gathered at the bank, with more people trailing over as we watch. Something must be going on, but I don't remember hearing about any gatherings. "I don't know. Maybe they're all trying to catch fish with their hands?"

Jorrin did that once. Just thinking of the memory has me torn between laughing and being in awe. It'd be a good skill for him to teach others. I wonder if I could ever figure it out.

"Hopefully they're more graceful than Felix."

I chuckle. If he were here, he'd be laughing even harder. Jorrin may be a good teacher, but Felix is isn't exactly coordinated.

Kaylyn heads toward the gathering, and I follow after, like usual. We're not the only ones coming, either. Others have spotted the crowd and are headed toward it as well. But no Jorrin in sight.

When we get in the midst of those hovering around someone, I ask, "Who's that, Tavo?"

I lean closer to hear his reply, growing warmer just by being near so many people. "Messenger from Crowin. Weird things have been happening at their village."

Crowin? I went there once with Mom a few years ago. The memory brings a painful twist.

"What sort of weird things?" Kaylyn asks.

"Animals have been acting as if a predator

is about, even when the villagers can't find one. Strange clouds in the forest by them have been growing bigger by the week."

"What type of clouds?" I can't even think of what a strange cloud could be. And growing bigger? Clouds come and go as they should, sometimes gathering to take up the whole sky, dotting it with puffs of white or gray. They don't stick around and grow bigger. Except... "The darkness you can only see at the top of the mountain?"

"Same ones. He said they're even stranger up close. Odd color. Don't ever blow away. Only grow thicker and bigger."

The statement shoots a tiny spark of fear through me. But why should it? I mean, what he's describing certainly is odd, but why fear it? There's no way to know the answer to that. I wonder if Jorrin does. He sometimes senses things others can't.

The Aster helps the messenger head toward the row of homes on stilts up the mountain side, and the crowd begins to disperse.

"Are they going to tell us anything more?" I ask Tavo.

"Yeah. They were talking about letting him get some sleep before that, though. Apparently he came straight here, barely stopping for a real meal or sleep. They'll have a gathering later tonight that anyone can join."

Not sure I want to know what they're going to say in that meeting. "I'm going to go eat before then. I'll see you two later."

"Want some company?" Kaylyn asks.

She would come with me if I asked, but her gaze is focused far off in the distance on nothing, as if she's deep in thought. Heavy thought. "Thanks, but I'm good. I'll see you soon."

"Are you coming to hear what they have to say tonight?" Tavo asks.

Everyone's certain to be there, but I want to go crawl into my bed instead and stay there long past time to get up. "Probably."

"I'll see you then." He gives me a grin that's dulled by the worry of the situation, but like he still wants me to know he's here for me.

And it's true. Even though Mother isn't here, I have to remember I won't be alone. Not that I always needed her, but she would have been there. But Jorrin will probably be going, too. I give Tavo a small smile back before heading toward the dining hall. Jorrin has to be inside by now. Unless someone from the crowd waylaid him with stories of strange, shiver-inducing clouds. Wherever he is, I'll find him.

I don't have to hunt much; he's at a table in the back of the dining hall by himself. The hall is surprisingly empty for this time of night. After seeing the messenger, food doesn't seem appealing, but I grab some corn bread and chili anyway, before joining Jorrin.

He nods. "How are things?"

"Oh, you know. Dirt and weeds. Felix had

an accident that needed some tending to. Nothing much."

"First time this month for him, isn't it?"

"Second, but there was enough blood to make Brilona nervous. Kaylyn fixed him right up, though."

"She's good at that," he says. "What happened to her? I thought you two were coming to dinner together."

I push the bean around my bowl. "She, um —Have you heard...?"

He stops eating. "Is everything all right?"

If I want to have a relationship with him, I should be able to tell him what I'm feeling. Besides, he's asking. That has to be a good sign. Right? "Have you heard about the messenger from Crowin?"

"No."

"Seemed like the whole village was down there to meet him." I quickly explain the few details I know, ending with, "Something about it has me feeling... off."

"That explains why it's so empty in here." He leans back, ignoring his half-finished plate. "There is something about this that feels different than other problems we've been called to help with. Though without Malryx, I guess it would."

"True. Even though I haven't been working with you guys much lately, I don't know how long it will take me to get used to them actually being gone." Maybe we'll never get used to it.

Maybe it's like archery. I've given it up, but it seems like it should still be part of my life. It's engrained in my every movement.

"You said they're meeting once he's rested?" he asks.

"Yes."

"We should be there."

"I… don't know. I'm not sure I want to be involved. I have to finish in the garden."

"Not at night, though. No one expects that. It'll still be there tomorrow. And I think if we learn more about what's going on, it will help."

Going definitely feels worse, but he's right. I need to learn about it. When have I shied away from anything hard? Never. Now isn't the time to start. "You'll come with me, then?"

"You know I will."

My heart flutters. I can do this then. He'll be at my side, and Kaylyn will be there. Mom must be watching me from the stars. Nothing could possibly go wrong.

Chapter Four

"Our crops are yielding less, our animals are fitful, and the darkness over us hasn't brought rain," Foley, the messenger says.

No rain? That's enough to drive a person crazy right there, not to mention the problems it would cause with food and animals. He continues talking about the village's circumstances, and the tales of how things have slowly been changing in the forest near them. How it slowly seemed to spread but didn't worry them at first—what was there to worry about? How things have gotten worse. How animals are acting strangely, and the dark cloud hovering nearby hasn't moved in weeks except to grow, threatening to block out their sun.

All of it makes me want to return to the garden, go back to before Felix interrupted.

If my mom was here, she'd have some ideas on what to do about it. The thought makes my worried heart ache. At least Jorrin's here, though. He looks on the scene with the kind of determination that makes me lean a little closer to him. Whatever is going on, it will be fine.

Suddenly, Kaylyn speaks up. "I'd be willing to lead a group back with Foley to see what we can find out and how we can help."

What? She's really willing to risk herself in this situation? I guess I understand. She's been struggling to find her place, and this is more like the missions we used to journey on together. Only, when my time as a Zophas ended, I was happy to be through—if a little lost for a while trying to figure things out. I wish she could be that way as well. What really matters is what the Aster and Astra think, the look they're exchanging. Whatever it is they read in that look, they both seem in agreement.

The Astra says, "This would be a good option for you, Kaylyn, and we believe your knowledge will be of great use with the task. We will find others to join you."

That's it then. She's leaving me again, only this time willingly. As the Aster and Astra discuss with Foley if this will work, I can't focus on their words. At some point, I slump back against the bench. The task is for a good purpose, but it shouldn't be happening. My father left, my mom left, Kaylyn's leaving. Everyone leaves.

"I'll go with you." Jorrin suddenly volunteers.

Point proven. My chest squeezes with a

painful twinge, but this doesn't have to be the end of us. Maybe it will be a good chance for Kaylyn, Jorrin, and me to spend time together like we haven't in too long. I stand. "So will I."

Kaylyn beams—not in the carefree way I do, but in her own subtle, glowing kind of way. Tavo also volunteers, along with a few other former Zophas.

"It's settled," the Astra says. "Gather supplies, and you will leave at first light. May the stars aid you on your quest."

As those gathered disperse, faces lighter now that someone capable is hunting to solve the problem, I slump back down on the bench. My volunteering was impulsive. Too impulsive. As much as I want to help, is it the right thing for me? For the others? The good thing to do isn't always clear.

It's been over a year since I've steadily served my Zophas calling. The time away from it has been better suited to me. As much as I'm ready to move on, Jorrin hasn't been away from the Zophas as long as I have. Maybe the time apart would have been good for him. For us.

More than that, the thought of this journey, and what Foley described, leaves a dark tinge of worry.

Chapter Five

It's peaceful this time of the morning and too early for me to be awake. I yawn as we start off. Kaylyn decided we should set off earlier than first light, so the stars still twinkle overhead, wishing our journey well. Foley is only too eager to get started. I, on the other hand, not so much.

"There's no sense in rising before the sun," I say, another yawn attacking me.

"You'd dance the night away and sleep all day if it wasn't for chores," Tavo teases.

If I weren't so tired I'd stick my tongue out at him. "As any sane person should."

"Right now is the best time to be awake," Sosha adds. "Night creatures are just going to bed and day creatures are just getting up. Sometimes you can catch glimpses of them both if you time it right."

"And your breakfast is still hot," Felix says.

"Fine. I'm the only one with a good sense

of when to sleep." I stretch as much as I can make myself with tiredness and the pack on my back weighing my limbs. "Thought the rest of you would have better sense than that since we don't have to go out on quests anymore."

"It was never the quests that got us up early," Sosha says.

"I know." A third yawn escapes me, making my eyes water. "I'm just lazy."

"I wouldn't say lazy," Tavo says. "More like you don't enjoy mornings as much as the rest of us."

In other words, everything is somehow the same as it was when we went on quests, even though it's all changed.

"Let's go," Kaylyn says, coming to our group and directing Foley to lead us down the dirt road.

Already, fading memories of past journeys make this one familiar, yet different. Jorrin is always near, though we don't talk. No one does. That our quest is something we've never tried before is too nerve-racking for chatter, I suppose. Not the most romantic way to spend my time with Jorrin, but at least we're together.

We continue on the full day, moving through the forest toward the mountains. We'll take a canyon to get between them, stopping only briefly for necessities and food. We break for the night and hurry to make camp and eat so we can be rested for another wearing day.

I stretch, letting the new movement combat

the day's soreness. "I've spent too much time doing gardening instead of stretching."

Jorrin laughs. "You should have joined me training. I figured even if I wasn't going to be a Zophas anymore, the exercise still felt good. And today it proved useful."

"I wish I'd joined you." This was the right choice—coming with. "Want to help me get firewood?"

"Sure." But his gaze isn't on me.

No matter. It's a good start.

☙❧

The second night we stop, there's more life in our group. The fire is big and bright, warming my face while my back is chilled. Though days are still hot, nights are cool. I'm grateful the melancholy from the first day hasn't carried on through tonight. When I don't think about it too much, it easily feels like traveling back in time to when we were all Zophas, fighting evil, and working together to make life better for everyone.

"We're running low on water," Kaylyn says to me. "I'm going to refill the waterskins at the stream."

"I can help, if you'd like."

"Thanks, but I'll be fine. Don't wait on me for dinner. I'll be back in a while."

Not surprising. She's always sought solitude more than I have. We may be like sisters, but I thrive with others while she prefers her own company. "Enjoy."

I do a few stretches outside the fire ring, trying to burn some of my nighttime energy while loosening my muscles so I'm not as sore tomorrow.

"Too bad you can't find this kind of energy in the mornings," Jorrin says.

"It's only too bad the rest of you don't have this much energy when we stop at night," I counter with a smile. "We'd have dinner in no time and still have a chance to dance and tell stories."

"But then your antics at night wouldn't be as entertaining for the rest of us," Felix says.

I laugh and sneak a glance at Jorrin, wondering if he has the same thoughts. He grins at me, the firelight dancing shadows across his face. Maybe he's growing more open to the idea of us. Everything feels perfect. Maybe he'll even propose before we finish this quest, and we'll have extra news for the Aster and Astra.

We converse as a group around the fire while dinner cooks. I've missed the smokiness, mixed with the savory smell of Tavo's latest meal. There's something so homey and comforting about it. The ache from losing my mom is tender at moments like these.

Jorrin stands.

I move toward him, my stomach jumbles in a way I can't tell if it's nerves or excitement. Probably both. "Where you headed?"

"Think I'll take a walk. Stretch my legs. I'll be back soon."

A clear statement he wants to be alone. The jumbles suck themselves into nothing. It's fine. Right? We've had fun. We're making progress.

"Soon, then."

"Yeah." Though his response is there, his gaze is already on the forest.

It's difficult not to stare at his retreating form, or wonder what he's thinking and what spawned his desire to be alone.

Once he's gone, the fire doesn't seem as bright or hot. The laughter is loud though, pulling me back to the center of camp which is surrounded by the darkened forest.

"We should do this more often," I say. "No reason why we can't get together once a week, have a fire, and enjoy each other's company still."

"Would the other villagers feel left out?" Azleco asks.

"Don't want that," Felix replies.

"Certainly not." Though it's hard to not want some time to just us. They'd be able to understand that. I think. I take a seat between Felix and Azleco, my energy finally sizzling.

After a moment of contemplation, Azleco says, "Perhaps we can talk to the Aster and Astra. Get their council on how to approach it in a way that allows us time without leaving the others feeling excluded."

"Fair enough," I say. "If we find a way, I

think we should plan to meet as soon as we get back." After all, I'm hoping to be planning a wedding shortly after that and will then want alone time with my new husband. "We could even catch squirrels for dinner like we had to for our first quest."

"And then let them go again," Felix says.

I laugh. "What? You don't like the taste of squirrel?"

"That, and I kind of feel bad for the little critters. They're kind of cute."

"That they are," Sosha says.

"First one to catch a squirrel and release it doesn't have guard duty," I shout.

We're all up at once, running off into the forest each in our own direction and hushing our steps once there. It doesn't take long for Sosha to shout out she's caught one. We gather around her as she releases the little guy, with some nuts as his reward for dealing with our antics in the first place.

"Guess there's no guard duty for you," I tell her.

"And you've just become my best friend for coming up with the idea in the first place."

I laugh. "If I am, then perhaps you'd be willing to take guard duty for me, since I'm exhausted from coming up with the idea in the first place."

"Of course I understand that, but no."

More laughter follows, proving this is still a happy place. Laughter and fun times abound.

It's good remembering what things used to be like. Gardening was a refreshing change after being a Zophas for so long, but being here makes me remember the good things that came with the calling. The friendships, the love, and the caring.

And Momma. I miss her. We weren't often on the same quest, but I still miss her presence around the campfire. She would have been like Kaylyn, taking charge of this situation from the start. What would she have thought of it? Something important. She'd have done something more than I've been doing. From this moment on, I should try harder to be like her. Still me, of course, but with some of her strength as well.

Tavo adds some dried meat to the pot. I pull out my herb satchel and move to him. The feel of the fire is warm and familiar.

"What flavor are you in the mood for tonight?" I ask.

"Whatever you pick will be great. You've got a knack for seasoning things."

He's too kind, like always. "My real knack lies with using these to help things like headaches, but I do know a little on how to flavor food. It's too bad I'm not actually a better cook, like you are."

"I guess we make a good team, then."

"I guess we do."

And it's true. As we finish making dinner, everything comes together smoothly. The smoky scent filling the forest, with the light of the fire dancing between the shadows, is a perfect reminder of how much I've missed this all. It's only too easy to savor the sensations as we dish up bowls for everyone and enjoy the meal. The others dive in eagerly as well, except for Foley. Too much must be weighing on his mind to eat. But I make sure he has plenty of food anyway and set aside bowls for Kaylyn and Jorrin.

When they return, they're together. As in, not just returning at the same time from a similar direction, but side by side. They didn't leave that way. Something strange twists inside me painfully.

Maybe they're talking strategy or some such. They did spend more time together in the Zophas than I did with them. They're used to traveling and working together. That's all it is. And it makes perfect sense.

As Tavo hands Jorrin the bowl I left out for him, Kaylyn returns the waterskins to their owners one at a time, saving mine for last. It means she wants to talk. Maybe I can get some insight into whatever strategy she and Jorrin were discussing. This feels more like home than I expected. It's time to do something more than just enjoy remembering how things used to be.

I grab her bowl and meet her at a rock away from the fire where we can talk a little more privately without entirely leaving the group. When she joins me, I can't help wondering what she's thinking. Her face is free of any telltale signs. I'm not entirely sure what I'm thinking at the moment, either.

"You and Jorrin were gone a long time. Anything interesting?"

She sits on the ground next to me, goose bumps prickling her arms. "We were talking about Crowin. I'm not sure what to expect, or what to do."

No strategy talk then, though close enough that the twist in my chest loosens. It's a different problem than we've faced in the past. How do you plan for the unknown? I give her the bowl I scooped out for her and grab a blanket from my pack. "You'll figure it out."

I wrap the blanket around her shivering shoulders.

"Thank you," she says. "And I should have taken you up on your offer to come with me. Then I could have left you alone with Jorrin."

The thought sends a pleasant hum through me that escapes as a laugh. "That would have been nice." Except I did offer to go, and he didn't seem to want my company. My laugh cuts off abruptly. "Sometimes I almost think…"

Her gaze on me suddenly becomes intense, searching the depths of my eyes for what I'm feeling. I don't even know what that is. Whatever thought was tickling me lessens.

"Think what?"

"It's nothing." Or mostly nothing. The tickle feels like it's still in the back of my mind, tugging and pulling, and any moment it could flare up, though I'm uncertain why. Enough dealing with the unknown. There's far too much of that going on already. "Any cute boys caught your eye yet?"

"When would they have had a chance to?"

Typical. I grab the closest throwable yet nonthreatening thing within reach, a leaf, and chuck it at her. Too nonthreatening. It drifts to the dirt, not even coming close to her. At least it sparks her laughter.

"Go ahead and joke about it for now. When a man finally captures your heart, you'll realize you're the silly one. Love doesn't need time. It forces its way into your life, whether you're prepared for it or not."

"It better wait to force its way in until later. There's too much to do right now."

Isn't that the truth? I can't help but peek at Jorrin, far on the other side of the fire and deep in conversation with Felix. "I wish it would have waited for me. Jorrin's always busy, like you, even though I've been struck by him. It'll probably be the same for you. Some handsome guy will make you swoon, even if you haven't got time for it."

Her shoulders stiffen as she sets down the now-empty bowl. "No time, and definitely no swooning."

"Oh, you'll swoon, all right."

Her nose scrunches as she laughs. "You're crazy. Besides, it's not like I'm going to fall here. Who would it be? Tavo, or Felix, whom

50

I've known my whole life? I could list every embarrassing thing they've ever done. The silent and worried Foley? No, love won't be hitting anytime soon. I'll have to stay on my own two feet so I can keep you on yours."

Always trying to take care of me, no matter what's going on around us. But it is good she's trying to keep me on my feet. Just being near Jorrin threatens to sweep me away from any good sense, and he's not even trying. I'm hopeless. But not as hopeless as the bush or roses we're sitting by. The colors are vibrant and cheerful.

"Do you see those roses?" I say. "They're gorgeous."

"They are."

It's getting cold. The air is growing colder with the deepening night. It's good to see a plant thriving while I'm struggling to keep warm. I place my hand on my pack but remember the blanket Kaylyn has wrapped around her shoulders is mine.

"Do you have your—?" Something skitters across my hand. A squeal escapes me as I yank my arm toward my chest.

Kaylyn is on her feet before I see her move, sword ready to take down anything. "What is it?"

A quick glance at my pack shows nothing. My nerves are taut though, stretched and pushed to a place I hate taking them. "I'm fine. Just fine. Something just brushed against my hand. It startled me."

Everyone gives me a look, except Kaylyn who's still looking around for trouble.

"It startled me," I tell the others.

Azleco chuckles, and without hesitation, Tavo punches him in the shoulder. Boys.

"What was it?" Kaylyn asks as serious as whenever there's a possible threat.

"I don't know." I glance at my pack again I but still don't see anything. I keep looking around and spot it. A tiny bird with its head tilted to the side. Its little beak opens and closes again without a sound, tiny feathers ruffled up.

There's a little blood on the sweet thing's wing, though it's hard to tell how bad the injury is without looking closer. It chirps at me, the spot of white between its eyes adding to its endearingness. There's no way I'm simply letting it continue through the forest in that condition. A predator could eat it. I softly coo at it and move slowly, trying to put it at ease as I cup it in my hands.

Its heart thumps rapidly against my palm as I turn back to show everyone it's sad, but still adorable, state. "I think its wing is injured."

Thankfully, Kaylyn puts away her sword. Or at least I'm thankful until she says, "I don't recognize it. Is it edible?"

Typical. She's never enjoyed wildlife like I have. No wonder the Aster and Astra are having a difficult time finding a task for her. I hum at the bird, trying to keep it calm, and ignoring her well-meaning but completely misplaced comment. "Its wing needs tending to. Anyone know how to do that?"

"I do," Sosha says, coming closer. I open my hands enough to allow her a better look without letting the bird free. She studies it a moment. "Not too bad. I'll fix her up. Then if she can avoid predators for a little while, she'll be able to fly again."

Quickly she gathers the items she needs from her pack and returns while the others wander off to ready for bed. Together we mend the bird. I only hope it's enough to let the poor little thing escape dangers until it can fly again. Everyone needs a chance.

Chapter Six

The night of fun is not repeated. We left it behind with the patched-up bird. If anything, things are weightier than ever, making me grateful there was at least some levity before everything became dampened by the clouds we draw closer to every day. Or are they nearing us? It's difficult to tell. They're not normal clouds. Low-hanging things heavy with dark dread.

The canyon we enter only makes the effect worse. Tall walls of rock on either side let in little light but still show the threat we're nearing. I try to keep things upbeat as much as possible despite the overwhelming sense we're going the wrong way. That those clouds we're moving toward are to be avoided at all costs. It's not the first time I've headed somewhere that felt that way. After all, it used to be my job.

"I've missed hanging out with you more," I tell Sosha as we walk together. "It's not the

same since we both went to help at the village."
Of course, she went a while before me.

"I've missed it, too." She sighs. "Working with animals is wonderful and a good way to help the community, but I miss our group. I miss the thrill that comes with fighting. The bonding that came with those long journeys. The others in the village, as great as they are, they just don't seem to understand things the same way we do."

"It's true. It's been good for me to see things differently, but it does make me miss our time together. There aren't the same chances to bounce and jump around like before."

"Do you think it will be like that again?" she asks.

I wish. "No. I don't think there will be a chance to go back, but things should grow and change in a good way as we get used to this." Though we've had time to get used to it. Maybe we just need more time?

Whatever we need will come. Though how can it now? We live in a world where everyone is at least good, if not perfect.

We continue talking through the day, stopping just once for a brief lunch. Though I wouldn't mind talking to the others, conversation with Sosha is easy and familiar. We resume our chat through the canyon until it opens up into what quickly becomes soggy ground. A swamp. Everyone's favorite.

We slog through it anyway, since it's the

most direct route. Foley pushes us all on as if his village's people depend on it. And quite possibly they do. The thought sobers me, but I push past it. No sense dwelling on the problem ahead since we can't fix it yet.

Kaylyn must not be fond of the swamp either. She slows, letting us quickly catch up to her. Both Sosha and I motion for her to join us, but with a shake of her head, she continues to let everyone pass her by. The fact she's worrying about what's to come takes more levity out of me, but what's to be done about it?

"You girls aren't as cheery as this morning," Tavo says, he and Felix joining us.

"Seems there's less and less to be cheery about," I reply.

"Come on now. There must be something." When no one responds, he says, "I know. The lying game."

"There's no need to practice that anymore," Felix responds.

"But it would be entertaining," I say, warming to the idea. "Who's going to catch the lies?"

Sosha says, "Tavo should. It was his idea, after all."

"Fine by me. Felix, you should start us." And give me some time to think of a good one.

"I'll give it a go." He grins. "I'm handsome. I'm quick. And I'm graceful."

I giggle. "Graceful is the lie, of course."

As the others continue to play the game,

Tavo catching them more often than not in their lie, I wonder what I can do to win the game. Before, it was always about trying to win so the others would be better at catching the Malryx in a lie. This is just for fun, but I still can't help but want to see how well I can do with it.

"You're up, Marsa."

My turn already? "I'm the best around these parts with a bow." I hesitate a moment before spitting out, "I'm happy. And I miss the Malryx."

"That's just too easy," Felix says with a laugh.

"We should stop here for a quick bite," Kaylyn calls out, halting our game.

All during the break, and through the rest of the day, things are more settled. Quiet. Things turn too heavy with the growing threat to start a new game, or to even finish the one we started. And the further we go, the heavier the clouds get.

Chapter Seven

The village is dark when it's finally within our sights. After the last couple of days of hard pushing, it's the last thing I want to see. The clouds in the sky don't seem like they can really be called clouds, but what other name could they be given? They're murky, hanging lower than ever. It wasn't easy to see them from home, but it was possible. Here, their presence is thick over the homes. If they became any heavier they'd fall the last few feet onto the village.

The thought makes my Zophasken shrink, curling tight inside me. Whatever that cloud is, I don't want it falling on me.

"Where is everyone?" Kaylyn asks, pulling my thoughts from the clouds, though I keep my eye on them even as I take in everything else. The way she grips the hilt of her sword hints at her concern even if nothing else does.

I grip my own sword as Foley says, "I don't know. The hall, maybe."

"Let's go then," Kaylyn says.

I couldn't agree more. The faster, the better. We all follow after Foley in a tight formation, like we're coming upon a group of Malryx trying to catch our backs unaware.

The darkness of the cloud is all I can focus on. It's wrong not to survey the area around me but so much more wrong not to shove my focus on the threat above. We're almost directly under it now. Whatever we must do to get to these people keeps us moving, going not just toward it but under it. The very air crackles with fear.

My skin prickles, and my hands quiver. We're going the wrong way. I can't help it. I stop. Only, the others stop as well, making my false move seem not as false.

"I think there are some people up ahead," Kaylyn says. "To the right a little."

Foley says, "That's the hall."

But we're all frozen. The next steps will take us under the murk. I want to tell them we need to turn back. That this isn't going to help the villagers. It's only going to lead to trouble. If Kaylyn hadn't already said there are people here, I'd speak up, but we can't leave them without the support we promised. The support they need.

Only, there's no way to save them from clouds and animals that leave a taint on everything.

Kaylyn is the first to continue on. Her footsteps are firm and sure, like there's nothing about the situation that bothers her. The others follow after, but the deep foreboding chilling my soul makes it almost impossible to take a step forward.

No one seems to notice my inner battle. How I force myself toward a place no person should be. I knew what I was getting into, or at least knew what was described, and that we'd be facing some sort of unknown peril. I didn't just agree to do this. I volunteered. I have to go on.

I must.

These clouds can't hurt any of us more than any clouds can, with lightening or flash rain or hail, and none of those have even happened. We'll all be fine. I will be fine.

As I stare at the back of the heads of those in my group, I will myself to follow them. To focus on them and not the taint above me, or the dingy, oily feeling that's grown as we've moved farther under them. It doesn't help. My feet just won't move, no matter what I tell them.

Tavo glances back, noticing my hesitance. Without a word, he returns and gently puts a hand on my arm. Its steadying presence warms me, finally giving me the strength to move on. After a few steps, his hand leaves me, taking some of the warmth with it, but leaving enough that I can keep going.

I give him a tight smile and stay close, fearing what may come if I don't. They need me here. I need to do what I can to be here. And maybe, just maybe, it helps him too. Maybe as a group, we all need each other to get through this. Except Kaylyn. She strides forward like nothing will stop her. Not even the darkness.

As Tavo and I rejoin the others, I realize they're staring at animal pens unlike any I've ever seen. Fat logs make up walls taller than any man. What type of animals could they possibly be keeping to need those?

Sosha is saying, "You need something so big to keep them from escaping?"

"Some jumped out of the fenced plot," Foley replies. "One even escaped after we built the pen higher."

Well that's just comforting. As if this place wasn't creepy enough already, crazed animals could be on the loose. If they're smart, they'll escape and run. I glance around as we continue on, hoping to spot the people Kaylyn felt with her power, but don't see anyone. We need to find them and get out. This place is not meant for the living. Though I doubt it's meant for the dead either.

Foley leads us to the biggest building we've seen in their complex, which must be the hall he referred to. He moves toward it, and I want to run past him and burst inside. There is goodness there. Even without stretching my Zophasken out, it's easy to sense in this gloom. I need to be closer, to feel it soaking into me. This place is too dark without it. I restrain myself, which is just as well, because when Foley tries to open the door, nothing happens.

Oh, joy. This place just keeps getting worse.

As he knocks, my hand twitches toward my bow like somehow it can slice through this air of gloom.

"Who's there?" Someone calls from inside the hall.

"It's me. Foley. I've come back with help."

There's a fat creak followed by the door flying open. A girl rushes out as quickly as I want to rush in. It's anyone's guess why she'd do such a thing, until she wraps herself around Foley with tears and kisses. "You're back!" she says between covering him with her kisses. "I was so worried."

He replies, but my focus is on the partially closed door, which lets out a slip of light, and the faint, soothing sound of murmuring. Of people filled with light and goodness. An ache consumes me, begs me to run inside, but we haven't been invited yet. The only person from inside is still focused on reuniting with Foley. Not that I blame her. They look very much in love. However, indoors seems like a better place to show it.

When the girl finally pulls him forward through the door, I rush after. The room is larger than I expected, crammed with people and homeware, like bedrolls and pots and pans. The soothing glow of people here takes the edge off my panic. The door slams closed, and a bar is laid across it with a comforting thud. I breathe deeply, taking in the clean air, free of murk.

The people around us don't look nearly as excited to see us as I am to see them. Their rather somber expressions are hungry, expecting something I'm not sure we're going to be able to give. Do they really think we'll be able to do something about nature?

Foley is glued to the girl who rushed out to meet him, gazing at her like he's never going to look away again, even as he talks to us. "This is Laynori, my betrothed."

Things make sense now. Why he was so eager to return. So set on moving us toward this doomed place as quickly as possible. As he introduces us all to her, and to the rest of those gathered, I can't help but think I would do the same for someone I love. For Kaylyn or Jorrin, or any one of the Zophas. Stars, I did it for these people I don't even know, though if I had known them, the same intensity as Foley's would abound. Of course, it's easier to think that when no longer outside.

He asks Laynori, "What's going on? Why are you all in here?"

Like that's hard to guess. Didn't he journey here with us? The village should have been stranger to him than to us. This isn't somewhere you'd want to stay out in the open, or even in a hut all alone. Only light and the company of others could possibly offer any comfort. But it's my time to listen and discover, not to have an opinion.

"The animals have changed. They've been

attacking us, even when we try to feed them. Attacking each other." Laynori's voice goes somber as she rests her hand on his arm. "A sheep got your dog."

"A sheep? Lucky was supposed to protect you. I should have taken him with me." Foley looks as if he's going to faint.

I can't blame him. I don't know what his dog was like, but just the thought of him dying confirms we need to get out of this place. Why isn't Kaylyn throwing orders at everyone to get ready to go? We need to move. Now.

Apparently, I'm not the only one who feels this way. Questions start from the villagers, flinging through the air, more rapidly with each second. They're desperate for help and comfort of any kind. Kaylyn doesn't give them an answer, and I can't understand why. There's only one clear choice. This is beyond us. We need to get these people out of here and report back to the Aster and Astra how truly horrifying this uncertain darkness is.

Chapter Eight

After a dinner that's not the best fare, but not the worst we've had to live off either, we gather for strategy. Why is it so difficult for Kaylyn to see we need to leave the foul place? It may be the villagers' home, but it's not something we can keep safe. Nor is it a place we should linger. Though the hall was a relief at first, the walls are already pressing in, the darkness lingering just outside.

Kaylyn has been silent since she called us together, her tightly pinched lips showing how deep her thought process goes. She must be coming to terms with the fact we need to leave. To take the villagers from this place. It can't be easy. Every other task we've been sent to had a way we could help. Even if we initially failed, there was something we could return to, to conquer later. There's no fighting the clouds, and though I suppose we could fight dog-killing sheep, it's not an action that will fix the problem.

"I think we need to go into the forest." Kaylyn's words wipe my mind of any thought. She continues. "If we explore it, perhaps we can discover the problem."

Or kill us all, including the villagers, without finding the source of the darkness. It's nature. What could the source possibly be?

"Has the water affected your brain?" Sosha's words mirror my own feelings, though more abrupt than I would have expressed them.

"No, it hasn't." Jorrin defends her in a soft tone. "What did you think we were going to do? Come here, look at the people, and then leave? She's right. The villagers don't know what's going on, and they've been here a lot longer than we have. They haven't learned anything by living here. How could we by simply visiting? They didn't know to look for a problem when the forest first started changing. We're going to have to go in, if we want to figure it out."

"Sorry I lashed out," Sosha says. "It's just terrifying."

Exactly. But maybe Jorrin has a point. Fine, he has a really good point. This is why Kaylyn is our leader and why Jorrin was a Zophas so much longer than I was. They can see the big picture better than the rest of us. But going in feels so, so wrong.

Though I will follow them anywhere despite the wrongness of it all, I can't do so without admitting, "I don't want to go in there."

"Me either," Tavo mutters.

"Do you really think we'll be able to learn anything by going in there?" Azleco asks.

"Of course," Kaylyn replies, sure and firm.

"What if it's just like here?" Tavo asks. Thankfully, I'm not the only one with these questions. He continues. "No answers anywhere but without buildings to protect us? What if there are animals that attack us like they did Foley's dog?"

As much as that would suck, being attacked is at least something we're used to. It's the feel of everything that frightens me. I bite my lip, trying to keep it all in.

"We know how to handle ourselves in a fight." Kaylyn reaffirms my thoughts.

"Not in a situation like this," Sosha says.

"Should we go right now?" Azleco asks.

Go home? Yes. Go into the forest? Please, not now when it's even darker than ever with night descending. There's no comfort from the stars when you can't see them.

"We should start at dawn," Kaylyn says, making me relax back against my pack.

"Do they even get light here?" Tavo asks.

"Tomorrow is good," I tell him, backing up Kaylyn. I can do that for her at least. "Be grateful we're not going tonight." I sure am.

Kaylyn clears her throat. "Anyone who doesn't wish to participate doesn't have to. We only need those who are willing to join us."

Just like they always used to say before

every quest, before heading into some Malryx's lair. There's always a choice. Usually an easy choice. But this time it's going to be a choice I don't want to make. We need to stay out of there. Though Jorrin and Kaylyn made their point well. No matter what comes, I won't allow them to face the darkness alone.

Chapter Nine

Kaylyn leans over to Jorrin and me. "Would you two please talk to the villagers? Foley, maybe, or another they consider a leader? Foley should be able to guide them back to our village. They need to go. Even if we fix this, they won't have enough food to last the winter. Make sure they know they'd be welcome, and that they will have help repairing their village once the problem is found and taken care of."

Even when I wish she was making another decision, instead of sending us into the forest, I can't be too upset. She's trying to help my relationship with Jorrin even in the midst of it all. The thought plaguing me, that we aren't supposed to be around whatever is going on, that no person should, is growing and needs to be addressed. We should be leaving with the villagers.

I lower my voice. "Are we really going to be able to find the problem and take care of it?"

"I don't know." Her voice is so, so tiny. It sends another wave of doubt through me.

She must have thought this through. As our leader, she must have considered all the options. Whatever happens, at least we're trying. I suppose.

Jorrin stands and offers to help me stand as well. The feel of his hand warms mine, but doesn't feel as secure as I'd like. There's too much pressing in on me to focus on what's finally right here next to me. The same problem must be plaguing him because his touch doesn't linger.

As we head toward the villagers, I take one look at how Foley is leaning toward his betrothed like she's the star in his life, and I know we shouldn't bother him. At least, not yet.

"Let's speak with someone besides Foley."

Jorrin's gaze travels to Foley, taking in the scene, and an expression crosses his face that looks almost like... longing. Something about it makes my heart ache in a fierce, jagged sort of way.

I hurry to turn to the first person we come to. A little old lady, frail and wrinkled, with short but big white hair and smiling eyes despite the circumstances. "Excuse me, ma'am," I say. "Who is your leader?"

"Aren't you a couple of sweet-looking young things?" Her voice cracks with age but is cheery. "You'll be wanting Deblin. I'll take you to him."

"Thank you," I say, and we follow her through the villagers as she continues chatting with us.

"So glad the Aster and Astra sent some nice young folk to help out. My own husband and children died in a fire years back, and I can never get enough of young kids ever since."

I place a hand on her arm as she turns to me. "I'm so sorry for your loss."

"Me, too, my dear. Me, too." Her heavy voice returns back to its more upbeat self as she continues leading us toward Deblin. "But that was a long time ago. Different trails than now. The Malryx that caused the fire are long gone where they can't hurt anyone. This crazed cloud, though. Don't know what to think about it. Couldn't have been happier when they welcomed us all to sleep in the hall. Though it's much noisier than I'm used to."

As she continues to chatter, seemingly happy to do so without a reply, I can't help but think on her husband and children. Their deaths were caused by Malryx. Probably not one I brought punishment to, her being much older than I am, but I did touch people's lives. Helped make a difference. Sometimes it's easy to forget how much good one did when their life changes.

"Deblin," the older lady says to a stocky man with a thin mustache. "These fine young people need a moment of your time."

"Of course. What can I do for you?" His voice is a high tenor.

As Jorrin begins to explain our needs, I hurry to thank the older woman who helped us before she leaves.

"Any time, dear. You just say what you need, and I'll be there. Come by my spot later when you have a chance, and I'll rustle you up a snack."

"That would be wonderful. What's your name?"

"For someone as sweet as you, I'm Granny."

I smile, chest light. "I'll be seeing you soon then, Granny."

Chapter Ten

Not long after we start talking to Deblin, someone yells that there's going to be a wedding. Usually a wedding is one of my favorite things. Being under the night sky, celebrating the union of a couple so committed to each other, they promise themselves to one another forever. It's a golden time, with much blissful celebrating. But tonight's marriage will be nothing like the others I've attended.

The stars usually shine down on the ceremony. Of course, sometimes a couple will set a date and go with it, whether or not the sky is clear, but usually they wait for the weather and not a day. But here, there is no unblocking the sky. There's no peace or joy in having the stars above us. Wherever my mom is up there, we can't see her, and it's unlikely she can see us.

She still would have celebrated this wedding, despite the darkness pressing in all around us, trying to sputter out our torches. She always said weddings reminded her of my father. Before he turned into a Malryx. Before the Aster and Astra confirmed he was a threat to our society. Mom wasn't the one to take him out by way of fire. All I remember from that day is her holding me tight and reading me stories. It wasn't something she liked to talk about afterward.

And here I am, thinking on it instead of the celebration about to take place. The black dinge pressing in on the moment has me more out of sorts than I should be. I take a shaky breath, trying not to think too hard on what I could be inhaling.

"I'm having a hard time breathing this stuff, too," Tavo says, joining me.

"It's unsettling, to say the least. Can't blame them for insisting on having it out here, though."

"I suppose." We're both silent a moment before he speaks up again, his voice quiet, but insistent. "Though to be with the one I love, I wouldn't mind how it happened. Tradition is nice, but love is stronger."

The words move through me, stirring something unfamiliar. But more than that, the intensity of his gaze and the depth of feeling glowing in him makes me want to lean forward. To somehow gain what burns so brightly in him.

"They're coming," Sosha says from somewhere nearby.

I jump back with the startling realization

that I didn't just want to lean forward. I was leaning forward. Though it didn't do any good. Whatever Tavo is feeling hasn't ignited in me. I glance at him to see if it's still there, but his focus is straight ahead at where the couple will soon be sitting. Not nearly enough of his expression can be seen to tell.

I have to force myself to focus on the center as well. To not lean toward Tavo or whisper to Sosha and ask if she's seen it in him, too. Even as the couple takes their place, sitting back to back on the floor of the roof, my thoughts can't focus on them. I can't properly think on their uniting being a permanent, good thing, like it should. Hopefully my pessimistic thoughts don't have a negative impact on their union.

The distance between the couple and those of us circling them is short enough we can support them as a community, but far enough to signify their reliance and support on each other first as a couple. The stars don't warm us, though. Instead, the taint of the darkness makes me cringe.

At least we Zophas are together. Kaylyn and Jorrin next to each other, across from me. Just their presence makes everything a little less tense. They're calmly watching the ceremony with real intent. Jorrin even has a faint smile.

The couple faces each other, taking each other's hands, and the two exchange their promises. These words aren't spoken loudly enough for anyone else to hear. They're for their

75

ears alone, but we're to witness that the exchange takes place. That their love is forever promised, in whatever words they choose to speak to one another.

Whatever Laynori says, Foley beams as she speaks—a spark in the dreariness of the moment. I can't help but think maybe it was right for them to have the wedding take place outside, after all. It might just be that their bright flame is what's needed in this darkness.

Their light grows as they begin the marriage dance. They move together, joy lighting both their faces. I can't help but think of the times I danced with Jorrin and wonder if we'll ever have a marriage dance. I peek at him, hoping to catch a hint of his thoughts, but he's so focused on the couple there's no telling what he's thinking—if it could be anything like what I'm thinking.

To my side, though, Tavo keeps glancing at me. Is he thinking of the conversation we had? Who's the lucky girl he'll get to dance with someday? With his attitude, I'm certain they'll be a happy couple, whoever she is. I give him a smile before focusing back on the newlyweds.

Once the dance is complete, those of us gathered around the circle cheer. Only not at the top of our lungs, as would be usual. The threat lingering over us makes it difficult to shout as loud as I can. It also seems like whatever this cloud above us is doing also makes it difficult to get the sound past it. Like it's blocking out joyful noise from going anywhere.

As the newlyweds end their first dance, some join them with a second. Others wander around and enjoy each other's company or find snacks to eat. A few, including Granny, climb the ladder back down inside the hall. I should join her and get further from the threat out here. I will soon enough.

Everyone is laughing and smiling in a way they haven't since we arrived. Except there's a hard edge to their expressions, an edge that says they're aware of the peril drifting around us at this very moment. That any time things could change. Nothing is known or safe anymore.

I move through the crowd, drifting in and out of the villagers until I reach Jorrin. He's by himself in a corner, gazing out into the black abyss. As I join him, he gives a half-smile, which warms and worries me at the same time. The weight of this is getting to him. It's settled in the lines around his mouth and the slight slouch to his shoulders, pressing with its dreary burden.

It's getting to all of us. Not even here a full day, and we're worn out beneath it. I almost wish it was Jorrin and my wedding happening tonight. There's no telling what tomorrow will bring on our journey.

If there will be anything after the forest.

The morbid thought leaves me shivering. It's just as well it's not our wedding, though. We haven't reached that point in our relationship as of yet. Besides, this isn't how I pictured my wedding to take place. Though it's not how I pictured my life either—to no longer be a Zophas.

"You're being sucked in by all this too, huh?" Jorrin's words startle me out of my morose thoughts.

My cheeks heat. "Hard not to be."

His gaze flickers to the bride and groom. "Even they seem to feel it, on what should be the happiest day of their lives."

I want to reach for his hand to comfort us both, but can't bring myself to move those few inches. What if he pulls away? What if the connection I've felt between us isn't what I think it is? What if the moment is too dark for me to make the first move? Best let him be the one to grab my hand, to show this is the moment. But I don't have to leave him wondering if I want him to make that move. I scoot closer.

Nothing.

Of course. That would be too easy.

"Weddings are happy days, even during circumstances such as these," I say.

"Good point," he replies, but he doesn't move closer.

I lean toward him further, keeping my back to the group and my gaze to the darkness. There's nothing else I could do to show that now is the time to make a move, without saying it or doing it myself. Still, he does nothing. Now must not be the time.

It never is.

Someone's gaze is on us. I look around just in time to see Kaylyn turning away. Why didn't she come by? She must want to give Jorrin and me the chance to be together alone. But the tight press of her lips said it was more than that. Despite all my teasing about love, and her insistence now isn't the time for her, maybe it really means more than she says. Maybe seeing all this makes her realize I had a point. No more teasing about love.

Tavo joins us, his face somber. Not even the wedding can touch his mood, it seems. As much I was enjoying his company earlier, I wish he wouldn't have interrupted the only time Jorrin and I've had to be together alone.

I give him a welcoming smile anyway. "Enjoying the festivities?"

"Not like I would have at home." He stares out at the darkness. "Lots of it is probably due to the situation, though."

"The situation isn't what any of us would like it to be," Jorrin says. "If you'll excuse me, there are some things I need to take care of."

"Viltruc."

Viltruc to you both," he replies and then is off into the crowd.

I can't help the sigh of frustration that escapes me.

"Have you told him how you feel?" Tavo asks.

"What are you talking about?"

"Jorrin. Have you told him your feelings?"

I open my mouth to protest, but Tavo's words stop me. "Don't bother denying it. It's plain to everyone but Jorrin."

Heat races through me, making the clammy air unbearable. Too bad it's not plain to Jorrin and a secret to everyone else. That's how it should be. Feelings. They belong up in the stars where those wiser than us understand how to deal with them.

"If you must know, I haven't said anything." If only I could be braver. "Even though I'm hopeful, there's every chance he won't return my feelings."

He scuffs his foot against the floorboards. "I know what you mean."

I playfully bump my elbow into his. "Ah, I see now. You have some hidden crush you've been keeping from us. Tell me, who is this girl?"

"Nobody who will ever know how I feel."

Something about the words twists inside me, but before I can ask him more, he follows Jorrin's path with the same down-trodden air. Why is it the two men who mean the most to me just walked off with no explanation?

Chapter Eleven

The walk is numbing. The forest black, clouds thick overhead. We've been walking for hours with no sign of day, despite being sure the sun should have, in fact, risen. We saw little of its filtered light this morning, but even that has been taken from us. What will we do without its light? Without the stars to guide us at night? The evil we fought as Zophasken was always dark, but there was light to balance it.

We shouldn't be here.

Now isn't the time to change my mind, though. I promised Kaylyn I'd support her, and I will. There's just something about this place, something about what's happening that screams at me to run the other direction instead of rushing off headlong into it.

It's only Tavo behind me that keeps me moving on, moving forward. The one good thing about this place being so dark—no one can see my shaking. It's violent and out of my control. I want to blame it on the cold, but it's not really cold. Every once in a while, Tavo whispers some words of comfort or strength. I don't know who it helps more, him or me. It'd be nice to think I'm not the only one this place is freaking out, but everyone else seems so unaffected by it.

Finally, we reach a clearing, and Kaylyn brings us to a halt.

"Why did you stop?" Azleco asks.

"I don't know where to go," she replies. "Everything has looked the same for the last several hours. I'm not sure we're still headed east. If it weren't for this clearing being new, I'd think we were going in circles."

Everything has looked the same. Bleak.

"We're lost?" Sosha asks. "I've never been lost before."

I have. Tavo and I once were lost for almost a week after raiding a Malryx hideout. The first and only time I've lost my sense of direction until now. I wonder if he remembers it, too?

"Should we split up?" Azleco asks.

Please, no! Right now I'm surrounded by them—my friends. They are the sole thing keeping me together. Keeping me sane. Keeping me from running, I don't care where to, as long as it's far from this place. And he wants to make us even fewer. Even if this is what we typically did as Zophasken, here it feels like downright blasphemy.

"We should stick together. We don't want to

make being lost worse by being lost from each other." Kaylyn's words have me holding back a flood of tears.

This place is tearing me apart. Threatening to rip me into shreds. I can't keep going on. Can't keep moving forward. "Maybe we should camp here for the night."

"It does feel late," Kaylyn replies, eyes darting around the clearing, even though it's difficult to see.

"And I'm hungry," Felix says in a somber tone. Even his spirits seem dampened by the pressing darkness. But he's still always hungry.

"We should use the space while we have it," Sosha agrees.

"Let's do it," Tavo says.

"It's settled then," Kaylyn decides. "Set up camp here. Everyone get to work readying us for the break. No one goes out of sight without a buddy. Even then, stay close. We'll eat and take shifts through the night."

The words shiver through me. I stick close to Jorrin and Tavo as we work to make a quick supper. Something light would be best, but we only have the ingredients we can keep in our packs. I don't dare try to scavenge for something to add to it in this dark world. Everything looks toxic. Black and deadly. I don't even dare sit on the ground without laying out a blanket first. Too bad I only have the one blanket and can't burn it come pack up time in the morning.

I wish the others would talk. I need something to get my mind off the chill creeping in, but I can't think of anything to say that isn't filled with despair, and everyone else is silent. We all push our food around. The couple of bites I've managed to force down churn my stomach with sickening heaviness. Food should never be this unsatisfying. I'm only too grateful when Kaylyn directs Tavo and Felix to save dinner.

"Let's get settled for the night," Kaylyn says. "I'll take first watch."

Usually, I would try to scheme a way to be close to Jorrin, but I can't even bring myself to care. I throw my blanket down close to Felix and Sosha and collapse on it. When Tavo makes a spot on the other side of me, it's easier to focus on the feel of them, the bit of light my Zophas can sense, rather than the pressing weight on my entire being from the air heavy with wrongness. I still don't let it out fully though, just relax it a little more, drawing strength from their presence to ease the tension.

"I'll take a watch with you," Tavo whispers to me. "If you don't mind. There's no way I'm taking a watch alone in this place."

I glance at Kaylyn, her gaze constantly scanning for trouble, face tight with resolve. How does she manage to be strong enough to do all this? To face the watch of darkness alone? I whisper back to Tavo, "I don't want to either. Thank you."

Chapter Twelve

Time to get up comes too early, though I can only tell it's time to get up by Kaylyn and Jorrin going around and waking everyone. The darkness somehow seems thicker than ever. Even though the others are still close, my Zophasken retreated back into its tight ball some time while I was asleep. I tuck it in tighter and turn to Tavo.

"I thought we were going to watch together?"

He shrugs. "No one ever woke me for a turn, and somehow I managed to sleep in this place."

"Yeah. Me, too. But no complaining about the extra sleep."

"Exactly. And, hey, there's always next time that we can watch together. Right?"

"Yeah, that'd be great." Anything not have to do it alone. Plus, I like spending time with him. He's such a good friend. "Looks like

Jorrin's getting breakfast together. I'd better go help him." Not that I'm hungry. In this place, it's doubtful I ever will be.

"Right." Tavo busies himself with the last of packing his things together.

As I help Jorrin, I can't help but wonder why Tavo went from being so friendly to closed off.

❧

I finish packing my things together and go sit next to Kaylyn. "You never woke me to watch."

"Jorrin and I watched all night. I don't think I could have slept. How did you manage it?"

So she didn't watch alone. I'm grateful for that. "It was easy to sleep when I knew you were guarding over us."

She looks away from me, ever shy about being praised, even if it is for what she was called to do. When she faces forward again, I pay closer attention to her. Something is off and not just the forest around us. It's something I've never seen come over her before. Her eyelids aren't just dropping from lack of sleep, but tight with worry. No, not worry. Defeat.

What happened to her last night? What does this mean for us? For this forest and the villagers?

I tread lightly. "What's the plan for today?"

Her continued silence isn't reassuring.

86

"I don't know," she finally says. Her face scrunches, as if in pain. Suddenly, she jumps up and runs behind a tree to where the girls have been doing their business. Only I expect that's not exactly what she's doing.

There's a pain in my chest, sudden and piercing, like whatever she has is affecting me too. I hurry to follow only to find her dry heaving. The sound tears at me, yanks, and shoves. There's no way to fix it here. No healing herbs to be found. No calm place to talk or rest. No cool rag to wash her face. Only this cursed thick air that chokes you as you breathe it in.

She groans, and I do the only thing I have left. I gently place my hand on her back. "Are you well? Is there something I can do?"

Without a word, she straightens and takes the waterskin I offer her with the last water from home. She takes a sip, not as much as she probably needs, but the tiniest smidgen of the strain eases from her. Can't think of a better purpose for it, but watching her drink it sends a twinge through me. Will we ever be home again?

She hands it back with thanks, but it doesn't feel as if I've done enough. I can never do enough.

"Is there anything else I can do?"

She sways, and for a moment, I fear she's going to crash into the tree. I reach out to grab her, but at the last moment she pulls herself upright, and my saving isn't necessary.

I've never seen her like this before. She's always so sure. So confident. The forest is breaking her. The darkness is crushing her. If she's the strongest of us all, what is it doing to the rest of us? What is it doing to me? When she finally speaks, the power twisted inside me trembles, confirming my worries.

"Nothing." Her words are crumbled in hopelessness. "There's nothing you can do."

Though she doesn't say it, I hear the unspoken—that there's nothing she can do either. We're doomed. We've come on a quest that's led down the darkest path we've ever known, only to have it be a useless journey. Can we even make it out of here alive? I don't know. I just don't know.

My fear stays tightly curled inside me. Jorrin or Tavo, or one of the others, I could tell all my thoughts to. I can usually say even more to Kaylyn, but not now. She needs strength from me. In these woods, it's something I don't possess, but I must act like I do. It's the first time I ever remember keeping my thoughts from her so specifically, but it's for the best. What I want to say isn't what needs to be said, but what needs to be said I can't say.

So I say nothing.

The tension that follows is laden with not just the oppressing forest, but guilt. It's sticky with my inability to be what's needed. It's almost enough to make me retch like Kaylyn just did. The churning in my stomach feels as if it will never have relief.

A moment later Kaylyn rolls her shoulders with a sigh and pulls herself upright, masking the fear roiling beneath the surface. I follow her the few steps to camp. Everything is packed, and everyone waiting for us, ready to leave and, from the looks of things, ready to fight, even if there's nothing left to fight.

Then again, I can't imagine what's out there.

The thought sways me closer to the middle of the group, bow ready so I can protect them, but the dark pressing in is still too much. I can't bear the feel of it, and the others seem bothered. The choking death is weighty on me. Do the others feel how strangling it is? How much it's trying to devour us whole?

The conversations are a faint murmur around me as Kaylyn gathers her things. It's hard to focus on any one of them until a voice rises above the others.

"Now what? We keep wandering around the forest?" Tavo's arm brushes against mine, warming me against the cold fear induced from his words. Fear I worried about since before we rushed into these woods.

"I don't think that will help," Kaylyn says. She scans us and the forest, her confident shield in place meant to bolster us, but definitely tinged with trepidation. "We should head back. We'll explain on the way."

Thank the moon! Tears prick my eyes at the

swarm of gratitude, but I blink them away. We can't leave this forest quickly enough as far as I'm concerned. If only we could actually make it out of here and not get stranded in this forbidden place. I don't know what it is—some vague feeling or impression—but it leaves me thinking that the forest doesn't want us to go. To escape its clutches. Or to even survive. And it's not going to let us leave easily.

Maybe that's what they're going to explain —that this forest has become a place of darkness no human should ever enter.

Instead of heading out immediately and telling us what's going on like I expect, Kaylyn continues looking around the clearing, her gaze raking through the forest like she's searching for something.

"Um... does anyone know where we came in at?" Her words tighten the worry gripping me. I've been lost since the moment we entered. If she's lost, how is there any hope at all? But there has to be some. One of us will think of something. We always do. The thought doesn't ease the grip around my heart.

"Great. Just great," Sosha says. "We're lost."

"And now we get to die in this freaky forest. Wonderful." Tavo huffs and scoots closer to me.

"Complaining won't help." Jorrin is the usual voice of reason. "Why don't we relax a little, and see if we can come up with a way to get us out of here?"

"Not like we can relax in here," Felix mutters.

Exactly.

The others put their stuff back down and shuffle around the clearing while my thoughts go to how I at least got some sleep last night, which says something. As much as Kaylyn is putting on a brave front, she's already admitted to not having been able to sleep last night. If I thought she might fall asleep while the rest of us figure this out, I'd make her, but it'd do no good.

"What's the problem anyway? What's wrong with this forest?" Tavo's words pull me back to the problem at hand, the one we have to fix, or Kaylyn will eventually have to sleep here. Maybe for good.

That's right! Kaylyn said she had an answer. Something she and Jorrin figured out. But her thumb is rubbing the hilt of her sword. It can't be a good answer.

"Jorrin, would you please explain it to them?" Kaylyn asks. "There's something I want to do."

"What's going on?" I whisper to Tavo. This is all getting weirder and weirder.

He shakes his head, like he's so confused by the event he doesn't even know what to say.

Jorrin heads toward Kaylyn and I follow, hoping for answers or at least a reason to fret less. The way she's acting is so bizarre. It's not

91

just the forest that has me worried now. She does as well.

"Do you have a plan?" Jorrin asks.

A plan for what? Finding our way out?

"Just something," she replies, staring at one of the blackened trees. "It's probably nothing, but I'll let you both know if I discover otherwise."

"Do you want help?" I ask her.

She shakes her head. "Thank you, but I need to do this myself. Jorrin, would you please let them know what's going on?"

Never before have I heard her ask someone to do something more than once.

"Of course." Jorrin's voice is strained. He doesn't like this any more than I do.

I stay at his side as we turn back to the group, inching closer to him as we go. Normally it'd just be because I want to be nearer to him, but now it's difficult to tell if I want to be closer to him or further from the raging dark.

The others lean forward, straining to hear the details to come. I'm as eager for answers as the rest of them, but it doesn't seem like enough. I peek back at Kaylyn, darkness brushing against my face as I do so. She's now sitting on the ground, sword in hand, with her pack still on, staring at a tree. What in the stars is she doing?

"…evil has moved into nature, taking over the job of the Malryx." Jorrin's words jolt through me, yanking my gaze to him.

"What?" My throat is closing in, as if it suspected before the air here was tainted, but now it knows for certain and refuses to take in another breath. I gasp for air as the others raise questions as rapid as my own, though more detailed. Nothing else can get through my throat. It grows tighter and tighter as I desperately try to fill my lungs.

Tavo puts a hand on my arm. "Just breathe, Marsa. We'll get through this."

His words help pull me through the terror clutching at my throat, but nothing can release it.

"How?" The word comes out raw and cracked.

"I don't know, but just think of the stories we'll have to tell after this."

"They'll certainly be unique." Though panic still claws at me, it's not as frantic as before.

"Maybe we can be traveling entertainers."

"I have missed seeing new places. Well, until now, that is."

Tavo's smile sobers, and Jorrin's words wash over me again. Evil in nature? How can that possibly happen? And if it has done the impossible, and it actually did happen, what can be done about it? Nothing we can do affects nature.

"Please let me explain," Jorrin says over the top of our noise.

The others settle down as we all focus back

on him. Tavo stays near me, soothing some of my panic, as Jorrin continues. "This is just a guess. We don't know for certain, but we think it's a pretty good guess. The strange happenings in the forest grew as the Malryx diminished, and now that they're gone completely, the darkness is overwhelming."

We can't do anything about this. Not just one village could be at risk. The entire world is in danger. "We have to tell the Aster and Astra."

"I know," Jorrin says. "And we will. We just need to figure a way out of here and then we can hurry to them. They'll know what to do if we can push ourselves that far."

The Aster and Astra will know how to handle this. A tiny doubt niggles at me, but I shove it away.

Suddenly Jorrin's face freezes. "What did she say?"

I realize he's talking about Kaylyn, but I don't know what she said either. The panic in his voice is all too real. Time slows.

He pivots and bolts behind us. "Kaylyn, wait!"

The anguish in those words rips through me. I turn to see Kaylyn touching one of those dark trees with her hand, eyes closed. I rush after Jorrin to help, to save her, to do something, but it's like everything is coated in hardened molasses. My legs can't move fast enough, though my brain still has time to process the horrifying scene. Kaylyn is trying to force her goodness, her Zophasken, into the tree. The tree that's a part of nature Jorrin just told us has turned evil. Turned Malyrx. And she's falling right into it.

Chapter Thirteen

Jorrin is yelling. His words don't register. The others are coming in a stampede of stomping. My muscles are bunched, straining to get to her. My actions feel useless, despite how desperately they're needed. She's shaking, like something massive is moving through her. My heart sinks.

By the time I finally reached Kaylyn, it's too late. She goes limp, landing in Jorrin's outstretched arms. Her gaze flutters up at him before her eyes close and don't reopen.

My own heart seems to stop. Her face is pale, her limp hand still outstretched to the tree, as if she's trying to heal it with her power. Something that can never be.

I slide to a landing next to her and Jorrin, trying to take off my pack. My arms are tangled in the straps, refusing to obey my commands. Someone helps me with it. Slides it off my back. Tavo. He hands it to me, already open, and steps back. Close enough he can help, but far enough not to get in the way.

I realize my hand is in my pack, grabbing supplies, and taking out pinches of several different herbs. I mix them with the last of the clean water. The water from home that she sipped not so long ago. Jorrin helps me open her mouth, and we trickle the liquid in. She swallows some, but nothing else changes. Without her awake, I don't know what to do. Gathering plants and herbs is my thing. I know which fixes what, but she's more of a healer in dealing with people. And what good would it do to see her power anyway? It's not like the rest of us have enough left to help her. We gave it all to her. And now she's in dire trouble. If she doesn't wake...

No. She will. She just needs time. Time. That's it. It had to be a shock to her system, nothing more. I grab hold of her hand as Jorrin cradles her in his lap, pulling her limp body close to him. I don't look back, but I can feel the others hovering nearby. We'll be lost if she—

Not going there. Not allowed. Ever.

My eyes burn despite my insistence, my chest a torrent of pain. I rapidly blink, forcing away the memories of losing my mom that are all too fresh, even though it does little to calm the agony building inside me. It's simply not possible for me to lose my almost sister so close after Momma moved on. Not possible.

But by the paleness of her skin, the faint

movement of her chest, I know it's all too possible.

The tears won't stop after that realization. The pain grows deeper, angry, and hurt. Kaylyn can't leave me. She just can't. I clutch her hand harder. Someone puts their own hand on my shoulder as I stare down at her too-white face, willing her to live. Thinking of her with every breath, wishing there was something, anything, I could do.

Suddenly she takes a deep breath. I'm frozen as she lets it out and begins breathing more normally, no longer faintly but with the stirring sound of someone trying to wake. The worry inside me is soothed, but doesn't entirely stop its hovering.

Her face grows a little pinker, though she's still awfully pale. If she's going to wake soon, I can't be crying. She always pulls on her brave face for everyone else. The least I can do is pull on my brave face for her and not betray how close to death she really came. She'll figure that out for herself.

Reluctantly, I release her, stand, and work on stopping the stream still pouring out my eyes. Tavo lets go of my shoulder, but his presence continues to stay close and offer comfort. Next to us, Felix and Sosha have tears streaking their faces just like me. As soon as I start wiping away mine, they follow suit. Once my face is dry and my tears fully blinked away, I glance back at Kaylyn.

Her head tilts to the side, closer to Jorrin, and he brushes the back of his finger against her cheeck. Something strange tightens in me then. Something foreign and definitely unwelcome. I push the thought aside while taking a step back.

The darkness of the forest seems denser now, like it's angry at Kaylyn for trying to force it to play on the side of goodness. Like it's ready to strangle us all with its sticky blackness.

I bite the inside of my cheek and peer over Jorrin's shoulder to see how she's faring.

She's awake, gaze drifting about dreamily. Then things come into focus, the light in her eyes dimming as she must be remembering what's going on. What just happened.

"Did it work?" she croaks.

Jorrin whips his hand away from her like the words physically hurt. "Whatever idiocy you were attempting failed."

Idiocy is right, but a strong word choice. Not like the Jorrin I know. But just like the Kaylyn I know. Trying to save all, no matter the cost.

She sits up with a groan.

"Take it slowly." Not that we have time for slow. Every second we're here is another second the darkness drips its sludge further toward us. But if we bolted for it now, not only would Kaylyn suffer for it, but we'd be lost in this terror of a forest. Hopefully, in the time it takes us to come up with a plan, she'll be rested enough to push on. If we can come up with a plan.

She stares at the tree she was trying to commit suicide by, a frown creasing her face. "I thought it might work."

"Giving your Zophasken to something not meant to have it in the first place? How did that seem like a good idea? At least you're not dead from that lunatic move." Though Jorrin's words are harsh, even if they're meant out of concern, and what she needs to hear, it's strange to hear something from him that would fit a Malryx more.

"Dead?"

"Yes, Kaylyn. Dead. Completely gone from us all. Didn't you ever pay attention to anything we were taught about our Zophasken, other than how to fight with it?"

I've never seen Jorrin this upset before.

"I thought the tree was like people.

"Shine it all! Sometimes you are so ignorant."

Despite all her hard work when it comes to defeating Malryx, she kind of is.

Jorrin bolts from her side, brushing past me as he hurries across the clearing. Hopefully, the distance will help clear his head, and his mind, so he won't give into the darkness surrounding us.

How would that be? Kaylyn is meant to defeat the Malryx. If he gave into its lure and became one, she would have to take him to the Aster and Astra. Possibly kill him, if his heart couldn't be changed. Would my feelings for him change if she did? Would they lessen? I brush the thought aside. It won't do any good now. Kaylyn needs me. I sit next to her, where Jorrin was only a moment ago, and hold my torch high, hoping to dispel the darkness enough to focus on the light and good.

"He's just worried about you. We all were." Because we'd be even more lost without her.

"I thought it would work. I thought I could fix it." She clenches and unclenches her hand around the hilt of her sword.

"I know, but it doesn't work like that. Plants aren't meant to be meddled with."

"What about the animals? Would it work with them?"

She really should have paid more attention in class. I suppose when you're the one chosen to defeat the last of the Malryx, other things are less important.

"They're part of nature. Nature can't be tampered with." If it could, would the Malryx have defeated us instead of being wiped out?

Before my thoughts can go any further, Felix comes up behind me and says, "It would have been a good idea if it wasn't for that, though."

Azleco also steps closer. "Thanks for at least trying."

Everyone else follows Azleco's actions. All except Jorrin. Whatever she does, even if it's a little misguided, we're showing our support of her. I reach over and give her hand a squeeze. My best friend. Our leader. Who we almost lost to this wretched place.

Chapter Fourteen

The gloom continues to grow as we try to give Kaylyn time to recover. Not that she's attempting to recover. Instead of lying down and resting for at least a few minutes, she keeps rubbing the hilt of her sword and sitting straight like a dagger is at her back, while muttering things I can't make out. Finally, I stand and move away from her. It's not that I don't want to help and support her, because I do. Of course I do. It's that it's too hard to see someone willing to sacrifice everything, even their own health, for an answer that may never be.

This place is like a Malryx's graveyard. And we're like the occupants, unable to leave. Forever to remain prisoners of our own bad choices. How long will it take to become an actual graveyard?

"Any ideas how to get back to the village?" Kaylyn finally asks, loud enough for us all to hear. "We should see what we can do to help."

How? Take them from their homes and hope the darkness doesn't follow us to our own village? Not that we can even do that. How in the sun are we supposed to save a village when we don't even know where we are? Why is she so focused on that? We need to help ourselves before we help others. It's the only option, and even then, we need to not just escape the forest but return home alive. The Astra and Aster have to be able to help, but if they can't…

"The villagers will have to evacuate, if what Jorrin told us is true," Sosha says. "But the Aster and Astra already said they could come live by us, so we know where to take them."

Am I the only one who realizes we don't even know how to get back to them? What's more, her words make me wonder if anyone else has thought about the fact that this darkness has been growing, seemingly moving faster and faster as time passes. The evil is spreading.

Suddenly, Kaylyn straightens in a way that makes me think danger is lurking. That Malryx is here. Which, of course, is impossible. I glance around anyway, but see nothing and sense nothing more than the danger that has lurked since we entered the woods. The one I wish we could have avoided. If only Kaylyn and Jorrin could have come to that conclusion before bringing us into the forest depths. If only their thoughts would have run along the same vein as mine. At least we know now. Continuing to wander this forest would be certain death. If not physically, death to our will to survive.

Kaylyn rubs her temple. I dig in my pack and pull out some willow bark and a cup. The coals from the fire are still warm, so I set the cup on them. I pour water into it, the only kind we have left—yuck— and use my knife to cut some ginger. I pound the ginger slices with the hilt of my knife and add them to the water. We're silent as it steeps. Who knows what the others are thinking? I'm trying not to think at all.

After a while, I take the cup from the fire. Tavo's ready before I even ask with another cup to pour the liquid into so it won't burn Kaylyn's lips. Once it's ready, I give him thanks and hand it to her. "Hope this helps some."

"Thank you." Her voice is strained, like her headache is affecting her words.

"Rest a minute," I say, as I start to clean the wounds on her hand from grabbing the tree.

"I'm fine."

Despite the fact I know otherwise—it's clearly evident in the faint tension lines between her eyebrows—I say nothing further. She finishes her tea much faster than she should, probably burning her mouth, and grabs her pack. At least the tea got down. It should give her some relief.

"No one ever did say if they figured a way out of here," Tavo says.

Not like we needed the reminder, but there is something. Something that Kaylyn's massive amount of power made me think may be possible. Only the thought of even attempting it myself first sends icy panic streaming through me. I should at least try it, but my power is so tightly wrapped inside me, desperately trying to stay away from the darkness. I just can't bring myself to let it out even a little.

But maybe someone else can.

"I may have thought of a way. If Kaylyn can do it." Luckily my voice doesn't quiver, despite the nerves running rampant through me.

"What is it?" Confidence is returning to Kaylyn.

"If you can stretch your Zophasken far enough, you should be able to sense people's light back in the village. You could use that to lead us back."

"It's a good idea." She gives me a faint smile.

Maybe. Maybe not. But right now, I wish she were easier to read. She wouldn't say it was a good idea if she didn't truly believe it, but it feels like there's more going on. Something jittery beneath her confident exterior. It could be the same hesitance as mine, only she's willing to risk anything to save people. I probably shouldn't have even said anything.

I glance at the others, who are all watching her hopefully. Now isn't the time to bring it up. If they weren't here, we could talk. Not that it would change her mind, but it would at least help me feel better about bringing it up in the first place. Instead, I'll just have to trust her and —well—hopefully we'll still be around to talk later.

"I can try. I don't know if I'll be able to reach that far." Honest again. Is that all that's bothering her, or is it something more?

"If you can't reach," Felix says, "we can give you more of our Zophasken."

I'd give it all to her if I thought it'd help. Just the thought makes my power tighten, wrapping itself taut around me. But I know I'd give it to her, even if it's scared to come out.

"None of you have more to give," Kaylyn says.

I force the words past my lips. "We have more."

Her lips twitch with tension but quickly relax so it's hard to detect. "It'll be fine.

In other words, she won't take more than she already has. She's been hesitant about it, starting a few months after the Zophas started giving it to her. Why, exactly, is something I've never determined. If anything, she should be grateful and honored, not scared.

"Just need a moment," she says. "I'll see if I can feel the villagers' lights."

I'm quiet as she focuses, not wanting to make it any harder for her. The others are too, all hovering closer together in the clearing. Yet, as the time passes, I can't help but be frustrated there's not more I can do to help. Maybe if I'd spoken up before we left, it wouldn't have come to this. It shouldn't have come to this. Not speaking my thoughts was wrong, and I owe her an apology. Probably to the others, too. Just not now. Not when she's trying to focus. When we get out of this forest, away from this oily air, it will be time.

The minutes pass, much too slowly. Not making a noise is becoming wearisome, my legs ache from standing still while they want to be not just moving, but fleeing, this place. Is this something she can even do? I don't know.

I rack my brain for other options, some other way to find a path out, but nothing comes to mind. Nothing. All our hopes of escaping this place hinge on her, and it doesn't seem she's having any success. I clench my fists and then cross my arms trying to hide it.

Tavo asks what none of the rest of us is brave enough to voice, "Did you find them yet?"

But there's no reply. Just silent Kaylyn with her eyes screwed shut, a wrinkle between her eyebrows.

This is it, then. It's really it. The end. My closest friends will be the last people I see. At least the end is with them. With Kaylyn, and Jorrin, and Tavo. Felix, Sosha, and Azleco. We've been through so much together—might as well die together.

How will it happen? Will nature turn us? Kill us with its choking darkness? Or just leave us lost and hopeless until we die of thirst or starvation?

Now would be the time to talk to Jorrin. If this is going to be the end, he should at least know how I feel. Or not now, exactly, but soon after everyone realizes it's futile. I glance at him. Take him in. The firm line of his mouth as he watches Kaylyn. Everyone is watching her. Everyone but me. As I scan the others, I realize that's not true. Tavo is also watching the others. Watching me.

He gives a smile that's not at all happy, but reassuring anyway. If our lives are going to end, at least he came with us. I forgot how comforting it is to be around him.

"I've got something," Kaylyn shouts, yanking my thoughts to her. "Let's go while I can still find them."

She really found them? We're really going to escape this place?

"Do you need a rest first? I hate to say it, but you look awful," Felix says.

It's true, she does, and a rest would probably help, but I'm already expecting her to turn it down.

"Thanks." She wrinkles her nose at him, and I can't help but feel the tiniest bit lighter.

It must lighten Jorrin, too, because he stops huffing to say, "He's right. It's a long journey. You should rest first."

"There's no resting in here. I want out."

No surprise, and I agree with her completely.

As Azleco passes her a torch, he says, "We'll follow you."

Kaylyn leads us, face fierce as if we were facing the known Malryx and not nature gone evil. I'm determined this time to not be in the middle, to be on one of the ends to help defend us from... Well, I don't know what I'll be defending from, but I'll at least give someone else a chance where it's a little more at ease.

Only, when the middle comes, Tavo motions me to go in front of him.

"I'll follow you," I tell him, though everything in me says I'll feel so much better if he's watching my back. Guilt pricks at me for being so desperate for safety.

"I insist."

I give him a grateful smile and hurry to catch up to Felix. Though they haven't gone far, the darkness is already fogging the air between us. How is it growing darker? Thicker even, like it's becoming more than simple air we breathe.

"Stay close," Kaylyn calls out. "I'm going to try to get us out faster than we came in."

We move. Not quite a run, but faster than a walk. The darkness slows us, trying to bind us to the forest. It feels like the journey lasts hours, but there's no telling how long it actually is. I falter, my legs able to keep going but my heart pounding with dread. Tavo touches my arm, and when I glance back at him, he gives a smile of encouragement.

It's something, at least. Something to hold

on to. His encouragement carries me on a ways, and he's there whenever it runs out, giving me more. I never thought about his actions so much before. How good he is at helping others. How good he is at being good. Jorrin always overshadowed everyone and everything else. Maybe love didn't have to be like that. Maybe I could have feelings for Jorrin, while still seeing the world around me. Perhaps I have been a little too preoccupied with him. Or, really, there's no perhaps about it. I *have* been too preoccupied with him.

In front of me, Felix goes flying toward the ground, slamming me back to reality. I reach toward him, but I'm too late to do any good.

"Are you all right?" Kaylyn yells.

Though he's usually slightly clumsy, and doesn't seem to mind, this time he jumps to his feet like the ground jolted him. He does what he can to brush dirt off him. I reach over to help, shaking the dirt loose with my gloves. The stuff is vile, dark, and almost sticky. It clings to my gloves and Felix, making my insides quake with fear. It's just dirt, I tell myself. Just dirt. Only, if nature's going evil, is it more than just dirt?

"I'm fine," Felix responds to Kaylyn, though it feels directed at everyone, as we finish batting away the last of the dirt. "You know me."

"Can we keep going, or do you need a break?" Kaylyn asks.

As exhausted as I am, taking a break would

be so much worse.

He replies, "I'm good to keep going."

Thank the moon.

Kaylyn gives an almost smile, before hurrying us on. It's only a few steps later when Sosha falls flat on the ground. And she is never clumsy.

What in the stars is going on? I move my torchlight, scanning the ground around me as Sosha takes hold of her sword and jumps to her feet. Nothing there that I can see, but Sosha falling...

Kaylyn asks if she's all right and gets a nod in response.

"Are you sure? We can take a break."

As much as I thought that wasn't a good idea before, and well, it's still not a great idea, it seems like something else is going on here. Something we need to be cautious about.

"I'd rather keep going," Sosha says.

"Let me know if you change your mind," Kaylyn says. "That goes for anyone."

Should I say something? Now would be the perfect time, but we're already on the move again. And what would I say? That I'm worried we suddenly seem to have a clumsy group when we're all just exhausted from being in this light-forsaken place? I'm over worrying. Again.

We move faster through the forest. And faster. Kaylyn is taking us so quickly, I'm afraid of tripping as well. Tavo puts a hand on my shoulder. He must have put his sword away. I'm not sure if the touch is to steady him or me, but either way, it's much better than running at this alone. Or as alone as I can be in a group of people I know better than I know myself.

The pace is frantic, my panting to keep up only fueled by the urgency to leave this place. The only thing left to hold me back is my own fear of falling.

There's another crash as Kaylyn flies to the ground in a graceful twist, sword angled away from Azleco. She's splayed out across the sticky dirt, sword tight in her grip. Azleco leans forward. At first I think it's to help, but then I realize he's focusing his torchlight on her. On something wrapped around her ankle.

It's thick and black and textured like bark.

Tavo brushes against me with a hiss of surprise. There's no way she could have tangled herself in a branch like this from what we witnessed. I don't even want to think what this could mean.

Sosha squeaks with fear. Jorrin tries to maneuver through us all to see what's caused the commotion. Even he freezes at the sight.

Kaylyn's lips tighten in a fierce line as she tries to get out of the twisted branch. All it does is cause her to hiss in pain. She lifts her sword toward it. She's going to end up cutting herself.

"Wait! Let me! I can get a better angle."

And keep her from chopping off her foot.

Her reply is to lower her sword. Something about talking in this place feels as if it will do more to attract the darkness. Not that I know how it would, but we don't know how any of this is happening.

I take a deep breath. This isn't something I can mess up, not unless I want our only hope of getting out of here without a foot. No way I'd ever let that happen to Kaylyn.

The bark is serrated, slicing into her ankle. The others squeeze closer to the trees to let me pass, hurry away from them once I do. I draw my sword and take a deep breath trying to calm myself. Trying to keep my hands from shaking. The thick branch is wrapped around her ankle, both ends of it flowing back into the ground more like a root. But how could a root possibly...?

No point in thinking on it now.

I gauge where the best place to hit it will be, close to her foot where the knot starts, but not so close as to maim her. I hope. Gripping the hilt with two hands, I raise the sword to my waist and bring it down on the branch with a crack. A small piece of bark chips off but otherwise no harm is done.

Kaylyn hisses.

"Are you all right?"

"Fine. Just finish it."

I chop my sword at it again, taking care to keep its sharp edge as far from her as possible, given the circumstances. Nothing. Wishing a bow would work for this task, I raise the sword above my shoulders, and Kaylyn closes her eyes. This time, when I come down on the branch—root, thing—it splits a quarter of the way through. The leaves in the forest around us seem to shudder, making a crackling echo around us.

The noise spurs me on. I swing my sword as quickly and carefully as possible. It takes three more hits to get her free. Three more than I'd like. The last strike sends a shiver of cool air to rustle the leaves and prickle my skin.

When the final blow frees her, she doesn't waste a moment pulling her foot away from the… thing. The wind picks up around us, intensity increasing with every passing moment.

Kalyn's ankle is dripping with blood, flooding me with guilt. "I'm so sorry."

"It wasn't you." She grits her teeth.

I gape at how much damage there is. What did it do to her?

Sosha must be thinking along the same line. "We need to clean that."

"Not now," Kaylyn replies, somehow bouncing to her feet. She takes her torch from Azleco. "Grab ahold of the person in front of you. We're going as fast as we can. Yell if you need something."

The wind cuts into me as I grab ahold of the pack in front of me. Kaylyn's pack. Azleco takes ahold of my pack and not a second later, we're off, running like our lives depend on it. It feels like they do.

There's no holding back like before. My

legs pump like I never knew they could. The wind grows brisker, swaying the branches around us as we fly past. One slices into my cheek, and my blood drips in a warm contrast to the icy air. The pain is sharp, intense.

Still, Kaylyn pushes on faster and harder, though it doesn't feel fast enough. The pain in my cheek urges me on even more so there won't be other wounds like it. The wind seems to reply to our quickened pace by going into a frenzy around us. Whipping about like a horde of angry Malryx.

Tavo calls out, though I can't make out the words. I'm slowing before I have time to think if I should or not.

"Tavo!" I yell, but the wind tries to carry it away.

Kaylyn is slowing as well, but Tavo shouts, "I'm fine. Go."

I grip Kaylyn's pack tighter just in time for her to push back to full speed. There's nothing that can stop her when she's in the zone like this, though I'd swear the trees are attempting to. Trying to not only stop her, but all of us. They whip toward us with frantic movements, like they're reaching their claw-like branches near us, wanting to puncture our skin.

My legs pump, burning with a strange mix of exhaustion and adrenaline. Kaylyn's pack bounces beneath my grip. One of the branches darts toward her, moving like it has a mind of its own. Even as terror tears through me, I lift my sword to block it.

Too late.

It jams into her shoulder before my sword whacks it away. She hisses in pain, but there's not time for anything else as another branch— even thicker this time—heads toward her from the other side. I'm maneuvering my sword to help, but hers is already lifted. She brings it down just as I'm swinging mine up.

As if it can sense our intention to maim it, the branch leaps forward before either of us hit it and wraps around her waist. The pack is ripped from my free hand as Kaylyn goes flying into the air with a warrior-like scream. She whips around the trees just out of reach, the dangerous bark surely cutting into her.

Shock freezes me in place.

"Kaylyn!" Her name screams from my lips as helplessness floods through me at seeing her tossed about like she's nothing.

A branch comes for me. Not as thick as the one that has Kaylyn, but I don't dare trust that it won't throw me into the air either. Ready for its rapid movements this time, I hack into it before it has a chance to take hold of me. Or worse.

It quivers under my hit, shying away before thrusting back toward me. I swing again, this time with enough strength to chop it apart. By the time I look back up at Kaylyn, she's soaring through the air, the flash of her skin the only way to see her in this dark place. I run toward where I think she landed, but another branch smacks against my chest with its length. Air gushes from me, searing my lungs.

Jorrin flies past, and then Felix, dashing in the direction I think Kaylyn went. Azleco sees me gasping for breath and hesitates. I wave him on, but he doesn't move until Tavo arrives. As Azleco hurries on, Tavo takes me by the arm and, together with Sosha, we dart after them.

Only, I can't dart. I'm slowing them down. My lungs still haven't recovered from the burst of air forced out of them. I can't keep the pace we were running at before.

"Just go." I try to wave them on. "I'll catch up."

"Like we'd leave you," Sosha says while Tavo moves his grip from my arm to around my waist.

We push on at a pace that feels dangerously slow, branches continuing to swing at us, all three of us working to keep them away. Keep them from injuring us further.

"Where are they?" Everything around me looks the same. Dark.

"Their light is this way," Sosha says.

There is no light in this darkness. She must be using her Zophasken to find them, but I don't dare let mine out to touch this yuck. We follow her through the forest as fast as I can go, which is faster with each passing moment.

With each step I feel a little better. Move a little faster. The forest is just as determined. It whips and lashes at us harder than ever. Sosha leads us toward the others. Toward light.

"We're close," she calls above the howl of the wind.

Moon bless me, I hope so!

A fat branch, bigger than the others, dips down and swings for Sosha. I jump forward, slamming my torch on it just before it hits her. The branch pulls back, smoking. I hear the others ahead of us. We've caught up to them.

And then there's nothing. The darkness is still there, of course, thick as ever, but the rush of trees is all behind us. We've made it out of the forest.

The lack of being thrashed is a welcome change, even if I still can't see anything. "The clouds must be moving faster and thicker if this is the village."

"They are," Kaylyn replies. "Much too fast. I'm glad we're all safe from the forest, but it's not enough. We need to get to the villagers and get home."

I don't even hesitate. I wrap her in a hug, tight and fierce. "I thought you were going to die."

She shrugs even as she hugs me back. "You know me. Even a tree throwing me around isn't enough to put me down."

"You're bleeding."

"I think we all are."

"Let's get moving then," Jorrin says.

"Something's not quite right," Kaylyn says. "Let's go see what's here."

119

"Can you keep walking?" Jorrin asks her.

She mutters something back to him I can't make out, then says, "We can assess our injuries when we're somewhere safer."

As a group, we quickly hurry over the land. There has to be a landmark here. A house. Something. Where is the hall? Where are the people? Why haven't they come out to greet us? To help us? Did we come out somewhere different? Somewhere there aren't any villagers? I try to ignore the horror clawing at me, threatening to overtake me.

Suddenly, there's a house smack in front of us, so close we're almost on top of it before we realize it. Thank the stars! "We're here."

"Sing praises," Sosha says while Felix gives a relieved chuckle.

"Everyone must still be in the hall," Kaylyn says. "Let's go."

As she leads us through the village I can't help but think it's quiet. Too quiet. The silence was heavy when we left, but this isn't just heavy, it's ominous.

I want to call out, holler at the villagers to meet us, or bring lights, or let us know they're okay before we get to them. Something. Anything. But the darkness digging into me has a strange sense of foreboding mingled in. A niggling that says the worst thing I could do right now would be to call out and disturb the silent darkness.

Soon, I realize Kaylyn isn't leading us

anymore, but we're all together, eagerly pushing toward where the hall should be. All hurrying toward what should be relative safety. Except for one. Kaylyn is behind us. Why isn't she as anxious as the rest of us? Why is she holding back?

Before I work up the courage to ask loudly enough that Kaylyn could hear me, Sosha says, "Finally!"

In front of me is the village hall, shadows dancing on it as the light of our torches flicker across it. Only, the shadows are dancing across a door thicker than when we left. More boards are hammered across it, but they're covered in scratches up to waist high.

Next to me, Sosha's arm holding her torch up wavers. "What happened?

"Apparently things got worse," Jorrin says.

"No surprise there," Tavo mutters.

The dark clouds make that clear, but it's not enough for a more reinforced, scared door. How much worse did it get? We all hover together, staring at the door, Kaylyn still bringing up the rear.

Azleco is the first to step up and knock. "We're back."

His voice is much too loud in the night sky. Or is it day? There's no way to tell. But his words must be loud enough to carry through the thick door. There's a scraping sound as the bar on the other side moves and it opens. I have to squint through, letting in a bright sliver of light to see Foley.

"Hurry." He opens the door wider for us, clutching it tightly.

I'm the second in line to enter, directly after Azleco. As soon as I'm inside, I flush at the warmth of those gathered. Not the heat, though that's there, too, but their goodness. It instantly soothes me. I hadn't even realized how cold the darkness was making me.

I turn back toward those still entering, wanting to make sure they all make it and are well. They hurry in and crowd near me, Tavo on one side, Kaylyn taking the other. Of us, Jorrin enters last, followed by Foley, who yanks the door closed and slams the bar down.

Next to me, Kaylyn staggers. I catch her before she falls to the floor, but only just. Blood soaks my hands. "We need medical help." The words shriek from me.

I lower her to the ground as carefully as I can. Tavo helps the last bit, yanking his cloak off and placing it under her head as a pillow. My pack is off before I can think, bandages in my hands and pressed on her seeping shoulder.

Her words slur together. "Jorrin. Jorrin needs help… first."

Behind me, Jorrin's voice is firm. "I've only got a little poke. I'm not the one bleeding to death."

"But I'm…" She loses consciousness before the thought is out.

"Stubborn to the last." Jorrin grunts. "Can

you fix her?"

"She's lost a lot of blood." And I don't know how to help. I barely assisted with wounds like this, let alone fixing them up all on my lonesome.

Granny is suddenly at my side. She moves my cloth aside long enough to glance at the wound, then puts it back. "Keep pressure on that."

I press down on it as she rummages through her own pack. "Bring hot water," she says to a girl no more than thirteen.

Granny moves quickly, readying a needle and thread far faster than I thought her gnarled hands capable of. "What happened?"

"You won't believe it," Tavo says.

"Try me."

"A tree stabbed her," I say, trying to keep my voice as steady as hers.

Granny grunts.

"And that was before it picked her up and flung her through the air."

At that, Granny pauses long enough to lift a single eyebrow at me, and she then quickly gets to work, making a poultice and pulling out more bandages. "Mad times are upon us."

Her words rumble through my head as she works. My hands obey all her orders, assisting her as best they can, but all I can think is how right she is. The Malryx were bad. Nature turned evil is worse.

Chapter Fifteen

Kaylyn groans in her sleep. I look away from Jorrin to check on her. It seems she'll be coming around soon. I want to talk to her, to hear her confident words, the undercurrent in her voice when she's leading that says everything will be fine as long as you listen to the plan and follow it. I don't just want it. I need it.

But not yet. Granny said it may take some time after all the blood Kaylyn lost. Granny had better be right. Kaylyn has to pull through this. We need her. I need her. She's my other half. My sister.

I turn back to Jorrin. "Do we need to tell them now?"

From the corner of his eye, he watches the villagers, but he doesn't answer or move from her side. None of us do.

After Granny finished fixing up Kaylyn, she and I looked over the rest of everyone's wounds, doing what we could for them. Nothing as serious as Kaylyn's. Mostly just deep scratches. Granny tends my cheek, and then she says she needs a long nap. I think we all do, but she certainly earned hers.

Kaylyn groans again. This time it's followed by the feebly moving of her hand as if she's trying to attack someone, or *something*, with her sword. She's gasping for breath. I check her pulse only to find it rapid. Whatever she's dreaming about, it's making her too frantic.

"Kaylyn?" I put a hand on her shoulder and gently shake her while trying to stay out of reach. "You're safe. I'm here. We all here, and we're all fine. You're going to be all right."

Her eyelids pop open, wide-eyed gaze darting about. When it meets mine, the darting slows, and slows further when she spots Felix. By the time she looks to Jorrin, she stops to stare at him. When she continues gazing, something in me gives a painful twinge. It's gone so fast. I probably just imagined it. Better yet, it's the situation getting to me. There's been too much going on for rational thinking and feeling. I mean, we were attacked. By a tree!

She tries to say something, but it's nothing more than a strangled noise. I grab my waterskin to hand her. "Sorry. We don't have any good water left."

She needed it too much when she almost died from trying to force her Zophasken into the tree. It feels like she needs it now, too. And she's not the only one with injuries. What are we going to do as they keep happening and we don't have good water? Because they will keep happening—I have no doubts about that. One more reason to return quickly. As if we needed another to add to the ginormous list.

Kaylyn's grip is weak around the pouch, and her first attempt to pull it back ends with water splashing onto the wood-slated floor beneath her. I place my hands over hers and help her lift it to her mouth. Despite it being the gross water, she eagerly drains the last of it.

"Careful. Granny did a good job bandaging your shoulder, but you don't want to take any chances."

The empty waterskin dangles in my hand, its lighter weight a heavy reminder that we'll soon be out of water of any sort if we're not cautious.

"Is everyone all right?" Kaylyn asks, despise my earlier reassurance, her words not quite their firm self, but closer than I'd expect them to be after such an ordeal.

"Yes." At least all right enough.

Her gaze turns into a distant look. "How long was I out?"

Felix replies, "Not long. Maybe an hour."

Her eyes pinch closed. "We need to leave. Now."

She bolts up, but I'm expecting it, and I already have my hand on her good shoulder,

126

gently pressing her back to the floor. "You need to rest and heal."

"Do I have any serious injuries?"

Thank the stars, no. If she did, it's doubtful she'd make it with only me and Granny here to help. But it means she'll push herself too hard. It would be so much easier if I could lie. "No. You lost a lot of blood, though, and have a lot of open wounds."

"So I'm only a little weaker because of blood loss from cuts and scratches."

Pushing yourself to do the best is important, but pushing when you need time to heal is suicide. For once, I wish she would just give herself a break. "We had to put a few stitches in your leg. You need to be careful so they don't tear."

Her gaze travels back over the boys and lands on Jorrin. She scans him, so I turn to do so as well. He's looking much better since he's had time to rest. There's no noticing his bandaged shoulder even though I saw Granny put it on.

"If he's fine, then so am I," Kaylyn says.

Maybe I should have hidden Jorrin somewhere else and avoided the question so she'd think there was an excuse for staying down longer. Not wholly honest, but it would have been for the greater good. Too late now. She's already brushing me off and sitting up. I want to encourage her to ease back down, but it won't do any good.

"Has anyone talked to the villagers?" she

asks.

Shame burns through me as I avoid her gaze. Of course we've talked with them, but not in the way she means. None of us wanted to leave her. I didn't want to. And how can we tell the villagers their home is being taken over by evil? I mean, we have to, but how? I don't even understand it myself.

"It's been an hour. What have you been doing?" Her stern words bite.

"Trying to make sure you weren't dead." Jorrin and I are clearly on the same page. Why can't she understand we just care about her?

"Obviously, I'm fine," she insists.

Felix adds, "Don't look at me. I'm trying to get used to not being the one everyone's hovering over."

My lips twitch, but I keep the full smile on so as not to aggravate Kaylyn while we're supposed to be working on whatever plan she's thought of. Clearly we've done a bad job of it so far, but I'd do it again, exactly the same way.

"Truly, I'm fine," Kaylyn insists, "but no one will be if we don't leave. Did they say if it's night?"

The villagers, she means. Which also means we haven't a clue because none of us thought to ask them.

"Azleco, would you please get one of the villagers? Preferably Foley."

Up and back to herself, and it's been less than five minutes since she woke up. No matter the injury, nothing can get her down.

Azleco darts away, and I can't help a little twinge of envy at the assignment. Now I know she's going to recover, I want some time to breathe and think. And thank Granny again. I owe her.

Kaylyn weakens once he's gone, just enough to show she's still feeling the effects of her injury, even if she's trying to push past them. "I feel like I lost a fight with a mad tree."

"You did." The thought makes me want to smile for some reason. Stress overload coming out in hysterics, maybe, but then I think of why she's here and why she's still alive. I glance at Jorrin, a flutter in my chest. "Jorrin, however, seems to have won the fight."

"I got stabbed in the shoulder. I don't call that winning." Despite his harsh response, there's a softening to his demeanor.

"You have fewer injuries than the rest of us."

"Only because Azleco and Felix were protecting us," he says. "Besides, no one else got stabbed."

"Any other wounds beside minor cuts?" Kaylyn asks.

"Nope." Though my cheek is still a bit bothersome, it's nothing like what these two have to deal with. "The worst of it is the two of you right here."

"Good," Kaylyn replies, and then says to Jorrin, "How did you find me in the forest?"

"My power is growing, enough that I could stretch it out to find you."

I should have tried to push mine out like that more, instead of being so worried about the darkness brushing against it. Even if it sucks, there's a lot it can be used for. Clearly. If we're going to get out of here, I'm going to have to be ready to do it. Who knows what our escape from here will bring?

"Thank you," Kaylyn says.

The silence that follows feels fraught with a tumble of emotions eating away at me. Why are things so hard? I don't understand this mess of feelings jumbling inside me. Things were supposed to be easier, not harder. What is it I need to do? And why do I feel like I'm intruding by staying with Kaylyn and Jorrin? The others are still here, except Azleco. Granted they're a few paces off, in their own conversations, but still. I should feel like I belong here. I do belong here.

Foley is at our sides, asking, "You wanted to talk to me?"

Kaylyn points at Felix's now empty chair, and once he's sitting, asks, "Is it night?"

"Almost midnight, but it's been this dark all day. The cloud cover moved over the rest of the village after you left."

"And the reinforcement on the door?"

"Something tried to get in a few hours ago." His voice is strained. "Don't know what, but it sounded unpleasant."

This whole conversation has me wishing I left when I had the chance. There's nothing really useful I can do to help.

"What made it go away?" Kaylyn asks.

"I don't know, but once we were sure it was gone, we reinforced the door. Good thing, too. It's come back twice, but not for a couple hours."

Why did it leave, and where did it go? I'm grateful it wasn't hanging around when we returned.

"We need to leave," Kaylyn says. "Now."

Finally.

Chapter Sixteen

Kaylyn said we'd leave in three hours. Just enough time to let the villagers get their few things together and do what we can to prepare for the trip. I insisted she and Jorrin get some rest. She's running on such little sleep, with blood loss and a wound to top it off. Hopefully she's not too upset that I didn't wake her half an hour ago like she asked. I almost did, but she was so gone, I couldn't bring myself to when we were doing everything that could be done. We need her strength when it's time for her to lead. I can help give her that, at least.

Some of the villagers are trying to convince Foley to let them return to their houses, but he doesn't think it's a good idea. Frankly, I agree.

"What if that thing, whatever it was, that came before, is still out there?" I gently try to remind them. "We need to focus on getting away from it as a group. I know your things are important, but how will you feel if people die trying to retrieve them?"

When one of the villagers starts to reply, Tavo says in a kind voice, "I know it's hard. Marsa knows it's hard. Foley knows it's hard. But you need to trust us. Trust her. Things out there are dangerous."

"But if we leave it, we may never get it back."

"A quilt my mother made. It's the only thing I have to remember her by."

My heart twists at that. If I was going to lose the only thing I have to remember my mother by, I'd want to get it as well.

Kaylyn strides toward us, eyes still heavy with sleep. The way she takes in the situation and straightens her back and shoulders, it's clear she still sharp enough to get some idea of what's taking place.

When she gets to me, she says in a voice for my ears alone, "What's going on?"

"Some of the villagers want to get things from their houses. We told them they should leave their stuff behind. We don't know what's out there, and we don't have time to get it."

Her lips tighten, the way they do when she's thinking. Only the way they're pinched until they've have lost some of their color makes me wonder if she's not just thinking but having something different in mind.

She turns toward the village members who've been begging to go. "You can go on three conditions. You move quickly. We are leaving in half an hour, no exceptions. You grab only what you can carry. Nobody else will be doing it for you. And you take one of us with you."

This means we're going to have to spend more time surrounded by darkness for things that are—well—just things. They may feel important, but the only thing that matters is staying alive and staying good. Even if I did have an object from my mom, I wouldn't want to risk getting it as much as I'd want it. I can't help but wonder why Kaylyn's giving into them.

Kaylyn quickly gives orders for us to go. The villagers must take her words seriously because they hurry to obey. While those who don't care about leaving their things behind finish readying, the few others gather by the door with all the Zophas.

Granny is in the crowd, a thick staff in her hands. I hurry over to her.

"I wouldn't be going, girl. Things aren't that important, but if you're going anyway..."

"Of course we can stop by your home," I say.

"It's not much. Just a locket my husband gave me when we were married."

Not worth dying over, no, but still of great importance. "Let me be the one to assist you, then. We'll move as fast as we can."

"And I'll do what I can to help it be a quick process."

She may look frail, but her spirit is fiery.

The staff in her hands isn't one I'd want to meet on a battlefield. Her force of will, her goodness, are even stronger. Exactly the sort of thing I want at my side in the darkness. Only I fear now her protection will offer me more than I can give.

I force such thoughts aside as Kaylyn orders the door opened and we file outside. We waste no time lolly-gagging. I hurry by Granny's side as she leads me to her home. It's not far from the hall, just a quick jaunt behind it, past a few other houses. I can't make out much of it in the dark, but what I can see seems well taken care of.

Except for the scratch on the door.

Granny runs her fingers over it, regret etched on her features. I place a hand on her shoulder, though I imagine having your home marred in such a fashion is hard to reconcile. She opens the door, and I give a quick glance around. It's a small, one-room house. A bed on one side, a table and a stove on the other, with a trunk and shelves that hold many personal items. Once I'm certain it's safe, I motion for her to go in while I wait outside. Just in case.

What could have left these scratches? And where are they now? I can only hope our presence will continue to scare whatever it is off. The world is heavy, though, dark with more than just the lack of light.

"Here it is," Granny whispers holding her locket in her palm. "My dear husband was always so fond of me. He was a Zophas, you know."

"I didn't."

"He helped train your mother, before he was released of duty, and we were married."

"I had no idea."

"I knew you were her daughter as soon as I saw you. Look just like her when she was your age," Granny says. "By the time I was married, I was already getting old while she was still a bright, young thing. Even then, she had great hopes that we'd finally be rid of the evil in our world."

"And look how that turned out."

"Yes, just look at it. Because of her and other Zophas's hard work, we now know what the world is like without Malryx. Evil is still here, only much harder to fight and contain."

With that, she closes her door and heads back toward the hall. It takes me a moment to trail after her. I was wondering if it was all a failure—getting rid of the Malryx, my mother working so hard to rid the world of the last evil person. But it's true. We do know now what happens. At least that much has come from it.

The task is done in less than ten minutes, and we're safe so far as we join the others on our way back to the hall. It's somehow darker than before, even with so many torches about. We stick together in a tight group, careful to hold our torches away from one another. The others join us as we pass or wait for us together in front of the hall. We're tight in our group, the Zophas keeping the villagers in the middle. Tavo is on one side of me, Sosha the other. It's not much farther to the hall door.

There's a rustle behind me. I grip my sword but don't pull it out. No reason to give Granny a heartache if it's nothing. Though her gaze flickers behind us, eyes narrowed. Laynori lets out a squeak.

"Did someone else follow us out?" Sosha asks.

"I don't know," Kaylyn replies. "I don't think so. I can't feel anyone else."

But the sound comes again. Felix yells, "Hello? Anyone there?"

"Quiet!" Jorrin says.

I grip my sword tighter, wondering if it would be better to switch to my bow. Jorrin wouldn't be so firm if there wasn't a reason. There's another rustle, this time to our left. As we move toward the hall, I take a step closer to Granny.

Suddenly, Kaylyn twirls around, gaze moving about rapidly as she scans the darkness. Following her lead, I search the area she's looking toward, but it's no use. Only inky darkness. The kind that makes me want to run screaming to safety. The hand gripping my sword starts to shake.

"Get in the hall." Kaylyn's words are soft, but firm.

We hurry the last distance toward the hall,

and the entire time I'm close at Granny's side, making certain she's protected. No matter how much I'm shaking, I'll do whatever is needed to protect her.

"Faster," Kaylyn calls out.

An old lady can only go so fast, though, and we are falling behind the group. Whether old and slow, or not, I'm not leaving her alone to whatever is out there that has Kaylyn and Jorrin so tense. For a brief moment, it crosses my mind to do what they're probably doing, to reach out and feel what's there with my Zophasken.

The thought of exposing it to the darkness, tainting it against what's out there, makes me squeeze it tight, safely inside me. Kaylyn and Jorrin are taking care of our group. I just need to do as they say and get Granny back inside where it's safe.

To the side, there's a strange growly noise. I glance to the right, just in time to see something launching at Tavo. My heart drops. My feet want to race to him, but I can't leave Granny unprotected.

Felix does what I can't, flinging himself in front of Tavo. The thing and Felix fly toward the ground, out of sight of the torchlight. Kaylyn's going for him. My heart rips in two, but I know he's in better hands with her. He has to be.

I don't need to prod Granny to the hall; she's already taking off without me. To do the duty we must. Keep those who can't fight safe. I hurry to catch up to her, sword out and ready in case another one of those things jumps out. The darkness seems to pulse with movement. My own fear pulses in response. What is that thing?

We're at the door, but not fast enough. There's another growl, much too close. Someone opens the door and ushers us all inside. The villagers hustle in, the other Zophas making sure they're in, while protecting their backs. I quickly inspect who's here and if anyone's hurt. Thankfully, nobody's hurt, but Laynori isn't here. She's picking herself off the ground near where the darkness makes it hard to see.

I dart out the door just as Tavo is carrying Felix toward the hall. Jorrin and Kaylyn's swords are swinging everywhere, flying toward the moving darkness behind him. Sosha jumps forward to help with Felix. He's in bad shape. Dark blood everywhere. My stomach lurches, the bit of food I had threatening to come up.

But it leaves me free to help Laynori. I rush toward her as she staggers toward the hall. Suddenly, a mound of darkness is on her, making them both fly through the air and land with a thud only feet from me. Her scream pummels the air. Even this close, I can't tell what the darkness is. I slash my sword toward it anyway, keeping it far as from Laynori as possible.

It shirks away from me before my sword connects. Another piece of metal flashes toward it. Jorrin. He swings in, muscles flexing as his swords hits it, dark liquid covering the blade. I wrap my free arm around Laynori's torso and pull with everything I have. I move her toward the hall, and Tavo comes out to help when we're almost there.

And we're in. Both of us slick with Laynori's blood.

Jorrin comes barreling in, yelling, "We're in. Leave it, Kaylyn."

His breaths come in sharp gasps. Kaylyn isn't coming. The thing she's fighting flies in at her, evading her sword, and bumping into her. She's going to kill herself out there.

If she won't protect herself, I need to give her something she can't refuse. I rush over to the still open door. "Kaylyn, please. Laynori needs you."

That's all it takes for her footwork to retreat toward us. The black shape attacking her follows, its form more solid than I first thought. What is it?

Jorrin and I hover inside the door with Azleco waiting behind it, ready to slam it shut the moment Kaylyn's through. I hold my sword up, pleading Kaylyn comes through first, without any more wounds. And then she's in, almost stumbling into us as she leaps forward.

The door slams with a harsh bang, a thud making it jolt. I dive toward the door, press my weight against it as another thud comes. It jerks me back several inches, but I'm there, back at the door, pressing with all my might, Jorrin and

Kaylyn next to me.

Azleco tries to lower the beam, but the door jerks again. We shove back, others jumping to help push against it. The clang of the bar coming down makes me sag against the door in relief. But only for a moment.

Everyone backs away, and I join Jorrin facing the door. The others keep their swords pointed at the door while I pull out my bow and notch an arrow. There's a thud. The door doesn't move this time, but how long can it last? I clench my bow, struggling to take deep breaths. Another thud. The door creaks.

I wait for a third hit. How much more damage can the door take? We'll be slaughtered if it gets through.

But everything is quiet. So, so quiet. Not the good type of silence that soothes and heals. The ominous kind. The one that says fear is what comes next.

Nothing comes. Still, the fear doesn't leave.

"Pile whatever you can against the door," Kaylyn says.

The villagers waste no time, bringing tables and chairs and shoving them in front of the door while we back up to give them enough room to work. Not far enough that we can't be ready if something gets through the door, though. When they're finished, Azleco surveys their work and gives Kaylyn a nod.

Sosha breaks the silence. "What was that?"

I lower the tip of my sword and keep my

gaze focused on the door—now hard to see through all the furniture—as I listen to Kaylyn reply, "A sheep."

No. That can't be. A chill sweeps through me as I think more on what I saw.

The villagers are muttering.

"A sheep did this?" Azleco.

Kaylyn turns toward where we left the two injured. Laynori and... Felix. It shouldn't have been him. But it shouldn't have been Tavo, either. It shouldn't have been anyone. None of this was ever supposed to happen. No one should be covered in blood, but many are.

Sometime during my morbid thoughts, Kaylyn has rushed to Laynori's side. I lower my sword, keeping an eye on the door. I just can't let my fear go. Can't let go of the fact that at any moment darkness can burst through that door in the form of something that used to be so innocent.

There's a moan, aching and hollow. I alternate watching the door and watching the scene unfold. Kaylyn is next to Foley, trying to comfort him as he holds his limp, blood-soaked bride. He yells, "She has to live!"

My chest is crumbling in on itself. As if the darkness is taking over, not just clouds and trees and animals, but the very world on which things are known. Such love they shared. It shone through them both at every passing glance. They shouldn't be separated. Not like this.

I sheath my sword and turn away from the

door. If something comes through—when something comes through—I'll do what has to be done, but right now, there's no help I can offer from here.

As much as I tell myself that, worry clings to me.

Some of the villagers go to Foley, while others comfort each other. No one is packing up any longer. No one worries about what can and can't be taken with us. Who knows if we can even leave? What will happen to us if we try? What will happen to us if we stay?

Granny is with Felix. I don't know if I can go to him, after all that blood. It has never bothered me until now. But I'm covered in it. His and Laynori's.

Tavo is at my side, guiding me to a corner where the water for the necessary is. He washes my hands. Scrubs my arms. Says gentle, soothing things. But all I know is Felix, covered in blood, and Laynori, ripped apart before my eyes.

Chapter Seventeen

Once the numbness wears off, I finish scrubbing myself clean and change clothes. Then proceed to scrub my clothes clean until Granny comes over.

"Felix is awake," she says.

"Is he going to make it?"

She purses her lips, eyes taking on a faraway look. "I don't know. Normally, I'd say yes. He has some blood loss but nothing more than what Kaylyn had. I've stitched him up, and he should be good as long as the wounds don't get infected. But something is... off. The bites those sheep gave him aren't like anything I've encountered before. I don't know. I just don't know."

I glance over to where the others hover around him and bite my lip.

Granny places a hand on my shoulder. "Don't worry too much. It doesn't fix a snotblasted thing."

The curse coming off her tongue so casually makes me snort, almost laugh, but things are too heavy for that. "I'll try not to."

"Let me take those for you." She grabs my dirty clothes. "I'll get them washed up while you talk with the others. They seem to be getting ready for some sort of meeting."

"Thank you. You've really done a lot for us since we got here. A lot for me."

"I'm only doing what anyone should."

Still, it means a lot. So much that I lean down and wrap her in a hug, heedless of the dirty clothes before heading off.

The other Zophas, including Jorrin, follow Kaylyn to a corner empty of people. Felix doesn't join us, though. A villager tends to him as he lies on a cot. As much as I want to go to him, I drag myself to the group, taking the last space to make a complete circle. Only it feels wrong after what just happened, to have anything be complete when Felix is so injured. I tilt my body to the side and casually rest my foot outside the circle. Not enough to draw attention, but enough to protest meeting without him.

Sosha is the first to speak. "What are we going to do? Are we going to be able to leave with that insane sheep attacking us? Is it going to maul more villagers if we try?"

Kaylyn doesn't even respond. Her face stays blank. No encouraging half smile. No determined set of her eyes. Nothing but a blank canvas. I've never before seen her like this. If she can't bring herself to react, what am I supposed to do?

"So that's it, then?" Tavo says, clearly thinking the same thing. "We're all dead. After working all our lives to rid the planet of Malryx, we're to die by starvation or sheep."

Starvation or sheep. Sheep! We've fought many battles—been confronted by foes so evil, they tortured innocents without a thought. Yet the strongest of the Zophas, those standing in this broken circle with me, are going to die at the hands of benign animals. Only that sheep wasn't benign. Not even close. I didn't think it would ever be possible to upset the balance of nature so grievously. I shiver.

Keep your voice down," Jorrin tells Tavo. "Focusing on the bad won't help us come up with any solutions."

"He's right," Azleco says. "We've got to figure a way out of here."

"We can fight off the sheep," Tavo says.

If Kaylyn couldn't, how could we possibly do it?

"Were you not there?" Sosha replies. "Those things are insane."

"I saw, but I know Kaylyn. She can get us past them."

He didn't see what I saw. Not the end when she was barely hanging on. When there was loss of innocent life, which we're sworn to protect. Life I was even more helpless than her to save.

As much as I love Kaylyn, now isn't the time to try to spare her feelings. "How? If Kaylyn couldn't defeat it before, how could she now? And what if there are more out there?"

My words send the others' gazes upon Kaylyn. Perhaps I should have thought of a way to say it without using her name. Though we'd probably still look to her. She's our leader. Only, for the first time, she seems like it's a position she doesn't know how to handle. I should have at least tried to give her more time. I still can.

Jorrin beats me to it. "I think we all need to step back from the problem. We'll take a few hours, rest up, and think of ideas. It's worked before. We'll come up with a plan again."

"But what if we manage to make it out of here and back home, only to find that this evil has taken over there as well?" Sosha asks.

I can't hold back a cringe. What if it does happen? The darkness was spreading before we came. It seems it only moves faster as the day passes. And now that we can't head straight home, could it beat us there? Our people will have no warning of what's to come. This is like being stuck in the forest all over again, only this time I'm even more aware of all we have to lose. All those depending on us.

"We'll deal with that if it comes," Jorrin says. "Get some rest and use that time to think. We'll meet back up in an hour."

Jorrin's words are calming, if not wholly reassuring like Kaylyn's usually are. The others start getting settled in the corner. If we're going to continue using this corner, I'm going to do what I can to make the best of it. I place my things as far from the walls as possible while not getting in anyone's way.

If the sheep attack, I'll fight them, but I can't bring myself to get closer to the darkness than I already have to. Knowing those monsters are out there only makes it worse. I'm surprised not everyone is trying to crowd in the middle of the room. I'm even more surprised when I see Kaylyn retreat to a far corner opposite of us— the dark one—void of people. Void of life.

Part of me wants to go to her, reach out, and be the support she needs. A bigger part of me says I can't give her what she needs right now. That I can't reach her. I can't even reach myself.

Chapter Eighteen

Once my things are settled, I disobey Jorrin's orders. It's for a good cause, though, so I'm certain he won't mind. In fact, he may even do the same. I wander over to Felix, pacing myself to expect the worst. When I reach him, I thank the villager at his side and let the man know I'll sit with Felix.

Once he leaves, Felix grins at me and tries to sit up.

"Don't get up."

"Oh, phooey. I'm fine. I don't know why everyone is so worried about me."

"Maybe because you just got slashed open by a sheep."

He shrugs. "Other than being really embarrassing, I don't see how it matters. Kaylyn and Granny got me fixed up real good."

"Other than the stitches."

"A few."

And something else. Something Granny

said about this wound being different than she expected. He does look pale. Much too pale. But he sits up despite my protests and grins at me, making my worries seem much smaller, if not disappear entirely.

"I missed you at our meeting," I say.

"I missed it. Did everything go well?" When I don't respond, he says, "I can tell it didn't just by looking at your face."

"There's just too much gone wrong with this whole situation. Far too much."

To my relief, he lies back down. "I hear you there."

After a moment, he closes his eyes. "Will you stay close?"

"Of course I will. I, or one of the other Zophas, will stay with you." I grab his hand, holding it like I would a brother's. "You just rest now."

He's softly snoring before I even finish talking. I watch his too-pale face for I don't know how long when Sosha puts a hand on my shoulder. "Why don't you get some rest? I'll sit with him a while."

I want to protest. I'd much rather stay here with him. Some of the color has returned to his cheeks during the short time I've been with him, but it almost seems too pink. Flushed.

"I'll keep a close eye on him. Granny said she'll be over to check on him soon. She was just hanging your clothes to dry. You need rest."

He stirs. "Go on. Get out of here."

I still don't want to go, but they're right. I do need rest if we're ever going to find a way out of here. Between Sosha and Granny, he'll be well looked after.

I grab his hand and give it a squeeze. "Don't go and tell too many interesting stories while I'm gone."

"You know I always save the best for you."

"Yup. You save them for me and everyone else you come across."

He makes a face at me, and I stick my tongue out at him. See? He'll be fine. The worry pricking my heart is just because of this mess we got ourselves into, not because of anything more.

I give my reluctant good-byes and go rest. Despite lying down away from the wall, the darkness still feels as if it's encroaching in on me. I doze, images of blood-thirsty sheep marring my rest. The memory of one flying on top of Laynori jolts me into a sitting position.

"Bad dream?"

"Tavo!" His name comes out more like a cry for help than a realization of who is talking to me. I cross my arms to try to keep myself together. "You could say that. That fight wasn't like any other I've encountered."

He scoots closer, voice low. "It's true. It was bad. Real bad. Fighting Malryx gave me nightmares, but this—?" He shakes his head. "I don't even know how to process this."

"You get nightmares, too?" I thought I was

the only one bothered by our fight.

"All the time. It's not so bad anymore, but they still come. Well, they'll probably be worse again after this."

"Yeah." We're both silent a moment. "I didn't think we were supposed to get nightmares. Not when we're doing what we should."

"I suppose even doing what's right doesn't leave us free from scars."

"Do you think we'll always be scarred?"

"I don't know, but I think we'll always have each other." His gaze is deep, like he's penetrating my thoughts.

"True. One thing to learn from all this mess if we survive is, no matter what happens, we Zophas stick together."

His gaze darts to the floor as he leans back, farther from me. "I suppose so."

The reaction isn't what I expected. I can't imagine what he wouldn't like about it, since that was what he was talking about. Wasn't it? I'm probably just imagining his withdrawal. There's too much stress here for me to think clearly, even if that's what we're supposed to be doing. Thinking.

I stand, and stretch, letting out my nervous energy. There's only one thing I've thought of that might get us home. It's probably suicide. No, it is suicide. But if it works, maybe it will give the villagers a chance to get home. If we're really lucky, maybe one or two of us will survive to lead them. Probably Jorrin and Kaylyn.

The thought of their names together makes me grind the soles of my shoes into the floorboards. Hard. What is wrong with me? Why am I suddenly struggling with this? Just because things haven't gone the way I wanted with Jorrin and me doesn't mean I need to twinge at the thought of his name linked with Kaylyn's. Does it?

I can't take the energy coursing through me. My legs are bursting to take me away. Only there's no away to go to. Everywhere, there's people. Children and adults, piles of packs ready to go, blankets, and worst of all, the walls the darkness is pressing in on. Am I making things up because I'm worried about the darkness so much, or are the walls tinted with black?

Tavo's next to me. I stop my rapid pacing as our gazes meet. The frenzy in me calms back to a more reasonable level.

"I didn't mean to run off," I say.

"That's why I followed. You seem stressed."

"Aren't we all?"

"Yes, but you faced more of that last attack than most of us."

I shiver.

There's movement by the ladder Kaylyn took. I glance over to make sure she doesn't need me. She's climbing down, her face more serene than when she left, and the tightening in my gut eases. At least until Jorrin climbs down the ladder after her. When did he join her? And what were they doing up there, on the roof, all alone?

Discussing our plight, that's all it was. They were Zophas together the longest. It's only natural they'd be used to working together on things. But if that's all it is, why is Kayyn avoiding looking at me after a quick glance? Why is she suddenly hurrying from one villager to the next?

"Hey, are you okay?" Tavo asks. "You've gone quiet."

"Just thinking."

He glances over to Kaylyn. "There's a lot to think about here."

"Yeah, but it's not easy to do. I feel like I'm missing things."

He takes a step closer, and the room grows warmer. He opens his mouth to say something, and I find myself leaning toward him like I need to be as close as possible to hear whatever he's going to say. But instead of speaking the words struggling to get free of him, he lets his gaze drift behind me. He shakes his head and clamps his mouth. I slump back.

"Looks like Jorrin is gathering the others together. We should join them." His words are sensible, but then why does he sound so resigned?

"We should."

Yet we linger, awkwardness making its way

154

into the stiffness of my limbs. I can't seem to dispel it. Can't quite make it away from the calm I've found in the middle of the room with Tavo.

It must affect him, too, because he waits with me. We're both silent, reluctant to move forward or back with words or actions. I can't help but think things should be different than they are, but I'm not entirely sure what those things even are. It's this place, affecting my thoughts.

He's the first to move. Once he does, it's only natural for me to as well, the stiffness growing more limber with each step.

When we join the others, there's a little bit of small talk, but almost everyone is watching the room. The walls really do look darker now I'm next to them. It's not just my worry, but something else, something more going on. The darkness outside is creeping in. And the sheep... are they still there? I wouldn't count on anything else.

When Kaylyn finally finishes talking to the last villagers and joins us, my body has returned to the aching worry, stiff with what's to come.

She and Jorrin converse a moment before she turns to us. "Jorrin and I have an idea on how we might get out. Did anyone else think of a plan?"

"Maybe. At least it's the best I could come up with," I say.

"What is it?"

"Simple. All of us go outside while we leave the villagers in here with the door closed. We stick close together and fight off the sheep. When we've killed them all, we go. If we work together, I'm sure we can do it. Give a chance for at least some of the villagers to make it."

And hopefully some of us will live. "It was hard last time because only Kaylyn was fighting them off."

"Can I just say it feels ridiculous to be talking so seriously about attacking sheep?" Tavo says.

All too true.

"What was your plan?" Azleco asks Jorrin and Kaylyn.

Jorrin taps Kaylyn on the arm with his elbow, and I can't help but wonder if that could have been me with him if we talked during the break. If our connection could be strengthened instead of theirs.

"We had an idea, too, that's a little different. We were thinking of having the villagers wait on the roof," Kaylyn says. "We'll rig a way to open and close the door from up there. The rest of us will lure the sheep into the hall. When they're all inside, we'll have someone close the door, and then get on the roof. The sheep will be trapped inside, whether or not we kill them. And, if we're lucky, there will be few or no injuries."

Of course. That's why she was going from one villager to the next instead of looking at me when she returned with Jorrin. Talking to them about a possible plan, not avoiding me. This place is making my thoughts crazy.

It's a good plan. Maybe better than mine. Though also more complicated, which means more chance for problems. Will the walls hold the sheep once they're trapped? Sure, they haven't gotten in here yet, but they haven't tried hard. Now they have us surrounded. They can play with us whenever they want. What happens when they're the ones caged in?

There are other things that could go wrong, too. I just don't know. Everyone else is agreeing to their plan, but I can't keep quiet. Last time I did, we were stuck in a forest and almost didn't escape.

"It's a good plan, but there are a lot more moving parts with it. Parts that could go wrong."

"There is a potential for problems," Tavo says.

"And it's likely the lures won't make it," Sosha adds. "Not that I mind giving my life for them, but it is a fact. We're already down on numbers with Felix being injured. The villagers are going to need at least two of us to get them to our home safely, I think."

"We won't need all of us in the hall," Jorrin says. "Just enough to trick the sheep into coming in."

Does he realize what he's saying? Tricking sheep? What are we doing?

"I can rig the door. It should help keep more people safe," Azleco says. "I think we should go for it."

"I don't like it," Sosha says, "but I agree. The sooner we get working on it, the sooner we can be out of here."

"Let's do it then," Jorrin says.

Kaylyn eyes me like she wants to know if I'm in support of it, but all I can do is shrug. With everything that could go wrong, I just can't give my full support, even if it's the best option we have.

Chapter Nineteen

The plan is complicated, like I expected. As Azleco threads the last rope up to the roof where a villager will use it to close the door and trap all the sheep in, I can't help but stare at the contraption he's made and wonder about it. Please hold together.

I go up to the roof and make final rounds among the villagers, assisting in settling those who need some place comfortable to sit and helping find children a doll or toy they can cling to during what is likely to be a noisy, stress-filled time. Many are frightened, eyes constantly darting out into the darkness. Though we can't see the sheep, we're almost positive they're still there. If they aren't—well—all the better. Not counting on it, though.

It's surprisingly silent with so many villagers crammed up here, which is as it should be. They were all warned to be as quiet as possible, and even the youngest seem to have grasped the seriousness of the situation. Not even the one baby of the village cries.

As I go, I look for Granny, wanting to find her a comfortable place to sit—something to ease her aged body. She's done so much for all of us. The smallest of her contributions, my freshly washed and mostly dry clothes, has still lightened my burdens. I want her to be as comfortable as possible, yet I can't seem to find her anywhere.

Everything else looks good up here. Hopefully it stays that way, no matter what happens below. What if the sheep have been watching us? It doesn't matter if they have; they're just sheep. Except they're obviously more. Not more enough to understand the trap we're laying for them, I hope. I scan the villagers again. At least those close enough to see.

When I circle around to Sosha, I ask, "Have you seen Granny?"

Her eyes twinkle with more amusement than I expect, though there's an undercurrent of steel. "She's by the ladder."

After giving thanks, I make my way back to the opening, only to see what brought the twinkle to Sosha's eye. I can see why she found it funny, but it makes my chest tighten. Granny is off to the side of the ladder, out of the way, but still close, a thick piece of wood that looks like the leg of a chair in her hands.

"You like it?" she whispers when she

realizes I'm staring. "A nice young, whippersnapper broke it off for me after I lost my staff outside. Should have something to whack those sheep, should it come to it."

Please, moon, don't let it come to that! "I think you could take on the world."

"But we both know you youngins will try to keep it from happening." She gives me a wink before growing more serious. "You be careful."

"I'm not doing the dangerous part. I'm just there as backup. It's Kaylyn and Jorrin who are really risking their lives."

"That may be, but you'll be down there just the same. Don't you go and take any unneeded risks. I'm counting on you carrying me whenever I get tired of walking to this home of yours."

If we weren't trying to be so quiet, if things weren't so serious, I'd laugh. At least the tightness in my chest isn't so unbearable. "And you keep yourself safely to the side here so I can carry you." More likely, Granny would be carrying one of the little ones with the way she carries on trying to save the world.

"There's some fight in these old bones yet." The words are hushed for the ears around us, but strong. Strong enough I'd trust her down there with us. "But don't you worry. I'll stay out of the way.

Tavo is helping Azleco with the last piece to open and close the hall door below. I give a curt nod to Sosha, who waits nearby, and she

161

returns the gesture. They'll be staying up here with the villagers, in case we don't make it. Not that I know what they could do past this point, other than prolong the inevitable. Death or injury by vicious animals.

Tavo finishes some knot Azleco had him working on, then stands, leaving us only inches apart. I start to nod at him, but before I finish the movement, his mouth is somehow next to my ear, our cheeks almost brushing.

"Stay safe."

Then he's gone. My skin feels colder without him. As I stare at him, he doesn't turn toward me. I shake myself and head for the hatch. He's where he needs to be, and I'm going down where I need to be. One of the best fighters, I belong down there. Tavo wanted to be with us, but I insisted the villagers needed the better of us two to stay with them, just in case. Kaylyn had to practically order him to do so, once she realized my thought process. He's not a Malryx, though, so as long as he understands my reasoning, I'm sure he'll forgive me.

Azleco offers me a torch, making me realize I've been staring. "For the fight."

"I'd prefer having two hands to grip my sword, or one free hand to grab my bow if it looks like I can use it." Unfortunately, in these quarters, I probably can't.

"I'll keep it safe for you, then, so you can use it when we leave."

My jaws clench together, and it takes work

to open them up again. "Thank you."

I climb down the ladder. Kaylyn waits at the bottom, Jorrin close beside her. When I glance back up expecting to see Azleco, there's Tavo instead. The thought of his quick words, his cheek coming so close to touching my own, does something to me. Lifts me up. Strengthens me. Steels me to do as he directed. To be safe.

And I'll do whatever it takes to keep Jorrin and Kaylyn safe, too.

I take my place by the bottom of the ladder as we agreed. Kaylyn briefly touches my shoulder. No words from her before a fight. All words have already been said. All that's left is her confidence in us. I can't help but wonder with the way she's been acting, if she's left any confidence for herself.

Jorrin follows her toward the door, but stops part way. He seems to lean forward, like he wants to follow her all the way to the danger. It's then I realize I'm doing the same. Despite being here only for backup, I want to be closer in case she needs more help. To not let her so near to the monsters.

Kaylyn shouldn't have the most dangerous job, when she's the one the villagers and Zophas need most *and* has an injury, but of course, she wouldn't listen. She holds her sword ready, torch glowing brightly beside her. She's a warrior, ready to give her all in defense of her people. And I'm her scared best friend, trying my best to back her, even when all I want is to

163

run beneath the stars again.

When she gives me the signal to have Azleco open the door, I want to refuse. To stop this before it starts. To make them see someone is going to die with this plan. Instead, I pass the signal on to Tavo.

A moment later, the door opens. The gloom seems to creep in with its presence clawing its way in like a deadly fog. Jorrin's torch isn't affected much in the middle of the room, but Kaylyn's light seems to dim.

All of my fears about the darkness are justified in that moment. I press my back against the ladder even as I grip my sword tighter. It's not just evil. It's trying to snuff out our goodness.

Other than the blackness pushing its way in on us, nothing happens. Though the encroaching darkness feels like more than enough, it's not the threat we need to draw out. My body stays taut, ready to move into a fight at any moment, but it seems the sheep no longer care about the hall. Or maybe my earlier thought was right. Maybe they saw us on the roof and know what we're planning.

A chill shivers through me. The open door now lets in not just darkness, but also cold. Is it trying to snuff out our heat as well as our goodness? Take out anything contrary to itself?

Jorrin takes a few steps forward, feet silent with the movement. As much as I want to help Kaylyn, I don't know how he can make himself move closer to that murk. Still, there's nothing. No response from the sheep outside. No hint they're even still waiting. Could they have left? Please, *please*, tell me they have left.

Kaylyn turns back toward us, gives Jorrin a quick scowl and then signals she's going outside.

She can't be serious? Go out into that—that dank existence—just to try to lure in monstrous sheep, which will attack anyway, if they're still there? Hopefully not. Hopefully she's just dealing with the yuck we'll all have to soon wander out into, but I don't like it.

I glance up at Tavo. His gaze is full of so much understanding and worry; I know we both want to stop her from doing this. But we won't. Because the villagers need to be certain it's safe.

Jorrin gets closer and says something to her, but I can't hear what. I'm certain it's about him wanting to go out instead. and Kaylyn refuses. Even without being able to hear them, it's not hard to guess where their thoughts are going. I've known them for too long not to know what they're both trying to do, using so much of that goodness inside them it almost hurts.

Jorrin plants his feet close to the door, refusing to come further back into the hall. Kaylyn shakes her head and then is out the door. At first I can still see her, though the gathering darkness makes it hard. A dim smudge of Kaylyn. Then it's just her torchlight. Then, nothing.

And nothing.

And nothing.

If she was attacked quietly, we would never know she was gone.

I shove the thought away. Of course we would. Jorrin is surely stretching his Zophasken out to follow her and track the sheep, but to me, it's like blindness. I could reach my power out right now and feel hers, if only it wasn't so tightly wrapped inside me, steeled against the darkness all around us.

Some friend I am. Can't even bring myself to force my light out to find her. Instead, I have to rely on Jorrin, on the fact he's holding himself stiff, but firm. Even in the murk between us, it's easy to tell he's struggling not to go after her, leaning toward the door again like he's using all his willpower to stay here. Once he lets that willpower go, I'll know I should follow, but it's worse not knowing for myself.

I stare at the door so hard my eyes start to hurt. It's just black on black on black. Nothing but darkness threatening to devour us all. Perhaps already doing so.

But then, in the darkness, there's a flicker, a flash that grows as Kaylyn flies in the door all arms and legs and sword with black sheep snarling after her. I get flashes of black and glistening sharp teeth as I ache to run toward them, but I have to complete my job, hand throbbing on the hilt of my sword.

Kaylyn reaches the middle of the hall,

Jorrin fighting alongside her, when she yells, "They're in!"

I holler at Tavo, but he's already gone, probably having heard her shout. I waver—stay at the ladder or help? I glance up again and still nothing. I'm about to give up and join the fight when Tavo's face appears.

"It's broken," he calls down.

Stars in all the ink that's holy!

The sheep attack Kaylyn, so many of them all at once, I can't keep track. Jorrin is hacking away at them faster than I can follow. I'm right there, legs having moved without thought, slashing toward the first black mass I come across. It snaps its sharp teeth at me, glistening with saliva that drips from its mouth.

"The door's not working," I scream.

I barely have time to register Kaylyn's growling response as I swing toward the sheep. Miss. I whip my sword around, slicing it on the nose as it lunges for me. As it retreats, another takes its place. It's like an endless swarm of angry black wool, all teeth and rage. My sword arm flies on instinct, years of training and fighting kicking in. Though all that training and fighting was never against a foe such as this. It feels like I will never swing my sword fast enough.

Still, with our help, Kaylyn's sword and torch have more room to move.

"Move toward the ladder as a group," she hollers back. "It's our only chance against all of them."

Maybe, but how will we keep them all in? They should have listened to me!

A sheep slams against me, butting my legs, and threatening to knock me over. I regain my balance, but only just in time to keep its teeth from sinking into my leg. Forget keeping them in—how will we stay alive until we make it there?

Suddenly Tavo's there, hacking at the sheep with his sword, torch in the other hand. He's like a graceful champion, scaring our attackers further from us and giving us breathing space so desperately needed.

The reprieve helps us all make it to the door in without dying. No idea if any of the rest are hurt or not. So far, the only thing wounded on me is my heart at not being taken more seriously about this plan falling apart.

Pushing my frustrations aside, I make one last swipe at a sheep and whirl toward the door. The others manage to keep the sheep inside while I shove the door closed and slam the bar down with a clang. The finality of it locking us in here with these things is haunting.

The sheep don't seem to have the same reservations, continuing the attack on us with a frenzy unmatched by any Malryx I ever fought. At least they're all in here now. The villagers can safely leave. Not that we'll join them. They'd better make it safely after all this.

Out of nowhere, Kaylyn bursts toward the

sheep blocking the ladder, yelling. She swings her torch while holding out her sword.

"Retreat now," she yells.

It startles me a moment, but then I run after her with Tavo and Jorrin. It seems to startle the sheep, too. Though they continue attacking, they seem confused as to whether to turn to us or Kaylyn. We make it all the way to the ladder as a group, continuing to fight as we go.

Tavo forces me first up the ladder and through the hatch.

As I rush up the rungs, I yell, "Don't you dare leave us, Kaylyn."

Tavo follows after me. The villagers within the ring of our torchlight are watching anxiously. If they weren't, I'd scream from not being able to help more. As much as I wanted out, Jorrin and Kaylyn are still stuck down there. How are they going to make it?

I hover out of the way but close by the hatch, next to Granny. She gives me a cursory check to make sure I'm not injured, but I hardly notice. My full attention is on this hatch. On the sounds of slaughter below—the growling and bleating, a cry of pain, heavy treading.

Jorrin's sword and torch fly through the trap. He climbs after, only to stick his head back down, arms stretched out. He's pulling Kaylyn up. No, not pulling. Throwing her out of that pit and tossing her to the floor of the roof with frenzied haste. I wrap my arm around her waist to help her off the floor to the side and out of the way. She leans on me, weight heavy. Granny immediately gets to work, looking her over.

Below us, the sheep grow angrier. Their growling, bleating, and thumps increase in frequency as Tavo pulls up the ladder. Only it's not so easy; it jostles under his weight, threatening to pull him over. I jump toward him, but Azleco and Jorrin are already there, hands on the ladder, shaking it with a curse.

"Throw it down," I yell.

And they do, shoving it down with such force there's a scream below. Did it hurt one? Are we safe from them for now?

Tavo slams the hatch close, face pale. When he sees me watching, he says, "They were trying to jump up."

All of me is icy, unable to move or think.

"I need a light. Someone bring a light!" Jorrin yells, and his panic makes me bolt to his side.

Sosha arrives the same time as me, torch in hand. The light shines over Kaylyn, struggling to be bright enough. I stay on the other side of it so Jorrin and Granny can see what they need to. Granny pulls back as Jorrin's movements become more frantic. More people with torches arrive.

"Where did it bite you? Where?" Jorrin is frantically running his hands up and down her leg, searching for an injury.

I hold my breath, taking in her battered state.

"I don't—it had my right foot." Kaylyn's response isn't reassuring.

I grab the torch someone is holding next to me, not bothering to ask or even see who I'm stealing from. It doesn't matter. They have to understand. I kneel at Kaylyn's side, holding the torch closer so we can see better.

Jorrin has her boot off in an instant and throws it to the side. Smooth pink skin over her shin and calf. The toes of her tiny foot wiggle. There's no sign of a wound. No blood. Hope starts to kindle.

Suddenly she laughs, and I can't help but sit back and let the torch sway a little. They didn't get her. She's fine. She was the last out of all that mayhem below, but she made it out unscathed.

I pick up her shoe, heart pricking with fear as I stare at the shredded bits. That was much too close.

"It didn't get you?" Jorrin says.

"Got her boot good, though." I show them the boot, hand trembling.

Jorrin's hands retrace her foot, especially her ankle, where her boot was shredded the most, and repeats, "It didn't get you."

"Guess I'll have to thank the cobbler when we get back," she says. "I always thought she did a good job."

I bite the inside of my cheek. That was too, too close.

"How are you going to walk around now?"

Sosha asks.

"She's still got two feet," Felix replies. I glance at him leaning on a villager close by, a grin on his glistening face.

Kaylyn gives a little laugh, and I can't help smiling, even if I still feel heavy inside. As if the sheep shredded my insides instead of Kaylyn's boot.

"You made it," Azleco tells her.

"We all did," Tavo says, looking directly at me.

I go to him. "Are you all right?"

"Just dandy. And you?"

"Same." Or I will be, once we get out of this place. At least the plan to escape the sheep worked without anyone getting hurt or ending up dead, even it did fall apart. The thought isn't lost on anyone as smiles and laughter flow over those gathered on the roof.

But someone needs to be practical. We can't stay up here forever. What if the sheep figure out a way to escape? With all their surprises so far, I wouldn't put it past them. We need to be as far from here as possible, and there are a lot of villagers to be lowered to the ground. "Before you go celebrating, let's get out of here first."

"I'm in agreement there." Kaylyn relents. "Just as soon as I can stand."

And we can ready everything while she gets to that point. I encourage them to get moving to the posts we established before the fray below happened and then come back to check on Kaylyn.

"I'm so sorry about the door," Azleco says. "I don't know what went wrong with it. It should have worked."

"Don't worry about it," Kaylyn replies. "You didn't have a chance to test it. We knew that going in, and we all made it out safely."

But we almost didn't. Almost.

"How are the villagers?" Kaylyn says.

"Scared," Sosha replies.

"Let's get everyone out of here, then."

"I've got the rope rigged up," Azleco says. "I'll double check it, and then we can be on our way. Marsa, could you help me?"

Sosha and Tavo are already leaving, moving on to help the villagers ready. I move to help Azleco but can't help but look back at Kaylyn and Jorrin. Together.

Chapter Twenty

My thoughts whirl together as I follow Azleco's instructions. Kaylyn and Jorrin and darkness and sheep and blood. It's all mashed together, like a nightmare I can't escape.

"I just need to tie this last rope, and then we'll be done," Azleco says. "Let Kaylyn know we're good, please."

"Of course." With my thoughts twisting through everything, I don't know if I want to talk to her right now. This is the first time I've ever felt this way. I go anyway, wondering if Kaylyn and Jorrin are still together.

When I reach an area where I can finally see them through the darkness, I stop, thoughts swirling back in on each other. Jorrin and Kaylyn are staring at one another. They're not just checking to make sure injuries are fine but gazing deeply into one another's eyes. The gaze seems to mean something more than what passes between friends.

I can't help but watch, even though I feel like I'm intruding on something. My stomach twists. What's going on with these two? It doesn't matter. It can't matter. At least not yet. Right now we need to get going. Even if it means interrupting something I never wanted to see in the first place.

"It's all ready." They bolt apart at my words. "And this time, he tested it out four times."

"Good," Jorrin replies, but he doesn't look at me.

Kaylyn tries out her shoe and thanks Jorrin before gathering the Zophas. "Let's go. If you don't have your packs, get them. Tavo, Sosha, Jorrin, and I will go first so we can help the villagers and guard them in case there are any more sheep out there."

"Do you think there are?" Sosha asks.

"I haven't felt any except for the ones trapped in the hall. We should be fine, but caution is still needed. Azleco, Felix, and Marsa, keep a close eye on the villagers up here."

"Of course," I reply.

"After the villagers are down, Marsa and Felix, you come and then Azleco. If there's enough light for you to jump down safely, you can untie the rope so we can keep it. If not, we'll have to sacrifice it."

"Let's go."

Black fleece, matted and covered in blood, flashes through my brain. We got them all.

Didn't we? We have to have trapped them all. We have to.

I help the villagers line up orderly, the strongest going out first, weakest last. Despite Granny's tough words, she's toward the back. Not only does her age make me worry for her, but her skills are vital.

Azleco helps them lower to the ground one-by-one. I keep a steady watch on them, helping keep their children calm, and telling them what to expect. It'd be easier if I knew. Everything I say sounds false to my own ears, even if it's what needs to be said. My thoughts are too muddled, the darkness more choking than ever.

I try to keep my mind clear of everything but the task at hand. I let it calm my movements and focus my thoughts. It's impossible to entirely forget the danger, which I shouldn't anyway, but it's even more impossible to ignore the crushing air, which I wish would happen. It's hard to even breathe, and there's a long journey ahead. Is this muck damaging us permanently in ways we don't even know about yet? How far will we have to travel before we get out of it? Will we be able to get out of it, or is it already too late? Have we already failed?

Where did that thought come from? No sense worrying about it now. Granny's right. Worrying is not helping anything.

By the time Granny's turn comes, there are so few villagers left there's not much to do. I keep a quiet conversation with her as Azleco readies her. Before she's lowered, she gives my hand a squeeze, her soft skin leaving me comforted even with that brief touch.

The last villager to go has already left this life. Laynori's body is already wrapped and prepared for cremation. I help Azleco secure the board she's on to the rope and slowly lower her down to the waiting Foley. The others watch in silence as he gently unties the rope and carries her somewhere beyond where I can see in the darkness.

My turn. I glance over the ledge. Those below are hard to see, the darkness blurring them. And that's what I have to go through.

I tell myself I'm in it now. It's all around. I can feel it. Everyone else has done it without complaint, even all the little children, but it's still hard to throw myself over the ledge and make myself move toward it. I've barely started down the wall when there's a movement of darkness out of the corner of my eye.

I don't think. I just jump. I fly toward the ground, flashing my sword near the black blur. A villager screams as my sword grazes the side of the sheep. Not nearly good enough. I thrust at it again and again, but it evades my sword with surprising deftness. Somehow it's even quicker than the others we fought.

And then it's on me. Legs pressing into me. Crushing me. I swing my sword up at it but can't get any leverage. It snaps at those who try to come close, but it doesn't leave its killing perch.

More villagers are screaming. I try to move my body, to force it off me, but its weight leaves me barely able to wiggle. My legs feel like they're being smashed as its saliva drips down onto my coat.

Not even enough breath left to scream.

A thick stick hits it on the side, pulling its focus away from me and onto Granny. No! I can't jump up. I roll onto my side, thrusting my sword toward its hind legs. Someone is screaming again, this time with growling anger as my sword connects and opens a deep cut.

The sheep jerks around, teeth near my face. I freeze, staring down those sharp teeth, covered in slime and foul stench. I am going to die.

Its eyes bulge, and it falls to the ground, a sword sticking out its side. Tavo pulls his sword from the carcass and kneels next to me. "Did it get you?"

Kaylyn is at my other side, pulling me over onto my back and tracing her hands along my body where the sheep stood. Everything feels tender. Did it break me?

Kaylyn grips my shoulders hard and searches me for a wound. "Did it bite you?"

"I'm fine. I'm fine." But I don't feel fine. I can still feel its feet on me, pressing into me, its spit dripping onto me as it lowers its mouth. I'm shaking, inside and out.

Kaylyn wraps her arms around me, easing some of my panic but making my battered body remember how much it hurts. Still I don't move. I don't say anything.

"I'm so sorry," she sobs. "I'm so, so sorry."

The way her tears soak my shoulder does more to calm me than anything else. Calm? More like shock me. This isn't the strong girl who's always led us. This darkness is tearing even the strongest of us to shreds. My body rocks with each of her sobs. I rub her back and make soothing noises as I assess the villagers around us.

They eye us with worried, panicked eyes. This isn't helping at all. It's making things worse. But Kaylyn never breaks down. She needs to let out her emotions. What is the worst thing I could do right now—stop her or let the villagers go unattended? I don't know.

"It's all right," I tell her. "All right."

She doesn't seem to hear me. Jorrin takes a step toward us, pain etched on his features, but then he turns to the villagers and starts talking to them, saying words I can't hear. At least someone is helping them because I can't leave her now. Not for anything. The way the villagers focus on him, the way the worry lines ease from their faces, I wish I could hear him. Maybe then I'd know what to say to comfort Kaylyn when there's no comfort to be had. But there's a small glimmer of the hope we so desperately need. That I need.

"It's done now. They're gone. We'll be home soon. Everything will be fine."

The crying eases. She gives a few sniffs. Her body relaxes, and she pulls away from me, her eyes filled with a light so cold I fear it will burn us all with its iciness.

"Kaylyn?"

"You're right, Marsa." Her voice is so detached it sends goose bumps up my arms. "Everything will be fine."

Chapter Twenty-One

We travel a ways from the village to have the ceremony. Granny insists Felix and I rest while they have the funeral for Laynori. I'd protest—after all, Felix is much worse off than me—but I haven't the energy to do it. Even Kaylyn seems wiped out; she sits on the make-shift chair someone got her to rest on during the funeral. Besides, the last funeral we attended was for my mom, and it's still fresh on my mind. It hurts more than my body.

I try to rest, but between the darkness and Felix's rising temperature, it's worse than useless.

"Can I get you anything?" I ask him.

"Don't worry about me. I wasn't the one used as a welcome mat."

"No, you were the one used as a shredding dummy."

He pffts at me, which would make me feel better if his eyes weren't so unfocused.

"Are you sure I can't get you anything?" I repeat. "Water? Food? Another blanket?"

"I'm really fine. No need to fuss over me."

Except for the need that comes of the worry this isn't the last funeral we'll have on the trip. It takes some time before the funeral is over, though not as much as they usually do. Tavo is the first over to us. After checking on Felix, who's now asleep, he turns on me.

"Do you need anything?"

"No, thank you." For some reason I feel extra shy around him now that he's saved my life. I don't know why. It's not the first time. We're Zophas. Saving each other's lives is part of what we do.

"I can't say you're welcome." His gruff response makes me gape. "Well, I can't. What were you thinking, jumping down from the hall like that?" Tavo paces away from me before coming back, his hand raking through his hair. "You could have been killed!"

He's never reacted so strongly to one of us taking a risk before. Not ever. "If I hadn't jumped, someone else could have died."

"You could have just yelled. Called out an alarm."

"There wasn't even time to think, let alone pick the safest course of action. Besides, this is what we do. Jump in front of others who can't protect themselves."

"Maybe it's not what you should do, if this is what happens to you." He stomps off.

182

He doesn't want me to risk my life? Just because I got a little hurt this time doesn't mean I shouldn't have done it. Or that I wouldn't do it again in the future. I'm tough. This is what my skills are for. Isn't it?

When I sit up, my body aches. Maybe Tavo did have a small point. I wouldn't be in so much pain if I'd just called a warning before finishing the climb down to help. I pull at my pack and grab some numbing herbs to take away the ache. It won't be long before we're walking, no matter what my body feels like.

"He just cares about you," Granny's voice comes from behind me.

"I know. He's a really good friend."

She grunts and kneels down beside me, age not seeming to get in the way of the movement at all. "Did you just take something for the pain?"

"I did."

"Good. Jorrin says we're leaving in the next half hour. Should give it time to help before we get going. You're going to be hurting a lot still. Lucky you didn't break anything."

"Lucky I was crazy enough to jump off a building, even if it wasn't the safest course of action."

"You know Tavo cares for you as more than just a friend?"

"What?"

"I've seen the way he acts around you. The way he looks at you. It's not the way someone acts who's just a friend." She stands. "Think about it."

And I do. I've always thought of him as just a friend. A really good friend. Could there be something more to it? Something I've missed all along? It would explain why he's overreacting to my trying to protect the villagers. Why he's always there for me when I need someone. Maybe Granny's right. Maybe there's more to his feelings. Maybe I've been blind to him.

Blind because of Jorrin.

What am I even supposed to do with that? With a boy I want to be with, who still hasn't shown interest in me, and another boy I've thought of only as a friend who apparently thinks of me as much more than that?

"Let's head out," Jorrin calls.

That half hour passes much too fast, and I still don't know what to think. I hurry and shove my blanket in my bag and join the others in the march to the forest. It hurts to move but not nearly as much as it does to think.

I'll put it off until later. My thoughts and feelings are so jumbled; I don't know what to do. Trying to make something happen to my love life on this trip was the stupidest thing I've ever done anyway. Why did I have to be so consumed with making a life with Jorrin that I couldn't see anything else around me?

Well, not anymore. I compel myself on, to do the job that needs done. Love can't be forced to happen, no matter how it seems to be moving along for everyone else. No matter how much I want to start a normal life and leave behind the stresses of being a Zophas for good, it's not happening, and I'm going to stop trying to press it. I'm going to just be me, and whatever comes with it, comes.

The moment we step into the woods outside the village, relief fills me. Not that the pressing darkness is gone. It's still there, crushing me. But we're moving, back toward where we never should have left in the first place. At least we're heading where we need to go instead of wallowing in the darkness.

The journey is much slower this time. Between the darkness and the villagers, it's hard to keep a rapid pace. They try, though. Carrying their children, quickening their pace at our urgings. Holding their torches high to light the way.

I keep my distance from Jorrin and Tavo both. From Kaylyn, too, though I'm not as certain why I feel I need the distance from her. When I'm not helping the villagers, I spend my time with Granny or Felix. Neither talks much, but then neither do I.

Felix grows worse by the day. It's not long before we stop to make a litter for him. I spend as much time assisting carrying him as I can. Tavo is often there. Sometimes Jorrin. Sosha and Azleco help as well, but usually it's some of the villagers who take turns to carry him.

His growing sickness urges us on faster

every day. There's only so fast you can go in the wilderness with a crowd—young children and the old. Trees and rocks in the way, the swamp was the worst of it. Water that burned when you touched it. But we made it through after a hard journey.

And all of it still in the darkness. The canyon is darker than most places, with the walls pressing in on us. When our torch lights up the stone, I see they've changed. It's obsidian-black rock now, edges sharp, though they seem to smooth out the closer we get to the other side. If only it means we're almost done with this journey and the light will soon find us again. But it doesn't seem like it. Everything is dark and dank, working against my sore, battered body. Will it never end?

Days and nights pass with a maddening blur. We don't even know if the nights are days, or the days nights. We keep at it, though. As I take a break from helping carry Felix, I move close to Kaylyn, wondering if now we can talk. Maybe it's time. At least I hope it is. I miss her.

"We're only a couple days from home. How are you feeling?" I ask, figuring it's as good of place as any to start.

"More energetic every day at least," she replies. "How about you? My injuries are healing nicely. You took a much harder beating than I did."

"I don't know about that."

"I just got thrown around by a tree. You got

stomped on by a crazed sheep."

"We've both had a crazy time of it."

She snorts. "That about sums it up."

Already things are going more like normal. Why did I wait so long to talk to her?

"Did you hear that?" Kaylyn says.

Nothing more than the usual sound of an entire village parading through the forest. "Hear wha—?"

"Did you feel that? Something dark is closing in on us from the left."

Just great.

She's calling out to the others as we both run toward the left. Sosha is gathering the villagers on one side, and I take the side I'm on. They don't need words. They gather whatever they can use as a weapon and hustle the young and the elderly to the center of the group. Except Granny, of course, who's stubborn as ever.

I pull out my bow and an arrow while I move in front of them, keeping close to Granny. Kaylyn and Jorrin both hunker down, weapons drawn, aiming toward the direction Kaylyn first heard the sound. After the villagers are readied, it grows quiet. The air is filled with dread of what's coming.

It's then I hear it. A sort of humming sound that darts somewhere close by. If I reached out with my power, I could probably feel it. It's circling around our group. The other Zophas and I move to protect the others from what's causing the sound, only it darts back. And around and around. It's toying with us.

"Don't follow the noise," I tell the villagers. "Everyone face the outside of the circle."

Kaylyn nods her approval without taking her gaze off the darkness and motions for the Zophas to circle round.

The fluttering sound continues around our circle, even though we're no longer all following it. Those using their powers must be struggling as well because they look wildly around as if they don't know exactly where it is. The beating sounds as if it's right here. What is it? And how is it getting around so quickly? It sounds almost like—well—almost like a bird flapping around. Except it's more like a drunk bird. A crazed, drunk bird.

Stars and moons!

I fling myself into the crowd of villagers, jamming myself against them. Once I've started in on them, they part before me until I reach the middle. The children and old ones. Just as I step among them, a small, dark bird darts from straight above, heading directly for a child not more than three.

It's too small. I switch my bow for a knife and stretch out. I miss cutting it, but the side of my blade knocks it off course. No time for relief. The villagers move almost as one, taking their sticks and knives to it.

They swat at the bird as it dives toward them.

But their movements are clumsy and untrained. None of them manage a hit, but the ball of blackness darts in and out as if it can't find a safe place to attack.

I'm about to move near it again when it hurtles back toward those in the middle. The weaker ones. I hold my ground to protect them; keeping eyes steady, finding its rhythm. Something about it seems familiar. It goes so fast it takes me a bit to find the bird, and it makes several more passes.

This time, it's prepared for my swing. It dashes away before I'm even close.

Kaylyn's working her way toward us, but the other Zophas look as if they don't know whether to protect the edge of the group or jump into the fray. The bird seems to spot our weakness.

"Scatter the children and elders amongst you," I call out.

"Quickly!" Kaylyn adds, though they don't need the prompting. The words are barely out before the villagers are moving to mix the weakest amongst them.

They're not quite quick enough. The bird darts, halfway between Kaylyn and me, right toward Granny.

A scream rages out of me as I trample over the others to get to her. She swings at it with her chair leg, but it dodges and goes straight for her face. When it hits, it's with violent ferocity.

She drops the club with a screech, hands

189

clutching a face that's already soaked in blood. The bird takes off just as I get there, but this time, it's not fast enough. My blade slices through it, ending its terror.

I stop only long enough to make sure Kaylyn's already making certain of its death. Then I'm at Granny's side. Though her screaming stops, the hands covering her face are dripping with blood.

"It's dead. Everyone's safe," Kaylyn calls. "Give us space."

The air around me empties of the crush of villagers. I take hold of Granny's wrists and whisper, "You're safe now. Let me look. Let me help." Inside, I'm swimming against a sea off failure.

"It's not so bad. Just my eyes." Her sobs are muffled.

Kaylyn's at her other side. "We need to see the damage so I can treat it. Please let me look."

Granny's hands only press tighter against her face. It's never hit me until just this moment how very thin her fingers are, covered with skin that sags and ripples with age. I place a hand on her back, tears streaming down my face.

"You can do this. I know you're strong. The other villagers aren't watching. It's just me and Kaylyn. We'll take good care of you." But there's so much blood. So, so much. And if it got her eyes…

She exhales a long, shaky breath, the kind that says she's about to do something she doesn't want to. When she removes her hands, I immediately turn away. It doesn't matter if I wince away from the sight. She can't see me. She'll never be able to see again.

I keep rubbing her back but stay silent so she doesn't know I'm facing away from her, or that I'm sobbing. There's movement, though, which must be Kaylyn hurrying to staunch the flow of blood. She's always deft at administering first aid, no matter the state of things, though I don't know how much her first aid will help or how much more Granny needs.

I continue to comfort Granny as Jorrin brings Kaylyn supplies and she finishes fixing Granny up. When I finally gain the courage to look back, Granny's eyes are covered in bandages, face pale beneath them.

"All done. We should camp here for the night," Kaylyn says.

"The villagers are already setting up," Jorrin replies.

Sometime during this nightmare, they did start setting up without my even noticing. Now they're almost done.

I tell Granny, "Let's find you a place to rest."

"Don't you go fussing over me too much now," she says and then seems to deflate, shoulders hunching in on her. "Though it would be nice to rest a while."

"Of course it would. I think we're all ready for that."

I find her a place to rest and make sure she's comfortable. I sit with her a while, talking softly with her until she starts to doze off. One of the women offers to keep her company while I get something to eat. I agree and thank her, but food is the last thing I want. Instead, I go to find that bird.

It's rather morbid of me, but I can't help it. I want to see the thing that attacked a person that's come to be most dear to me and left her blind the rest of her life. Besides, there was just something about it...

It doesn't take long to find. Kaylyn and Tavo are hovering over it. Studying it. Guess I'm not the only one who's curious. Before I come to a stop, Kaylyn stands. "I need to check on a few things. I'll see you two later."

I give her a good-bye, more focused on the bird than what she's doing. Tavo shifts, blocking my view.

"What are you doing? I came over here to see it."

"You don't need to, Marsa." His voice is soft and gentle but not what I need right now.

"It doesn't matter if I need to or not. I'm going to see it."

He stands, putting his hands on my shoulders. "If you're so determined. But you need to know it's not your fault."

I purse my lips, wondering how he knows I'm blaming myself. For not being quick enough to get to Granny. For not being able to save her sight.

"Don't look at me like that," he says. "It isn't. No matter what you learn in the next few minutes."

The next few minutes? What could possibly make my guilt worse? "What are you talking about?"

"Are you sure you need to see the bird? That you need to do this?"

"Of course I am. Something about it... I don't know. It's just, something seemed oddly familiar about it. Which is crazy, right? I've never come across a bird attacking like that before." His hands tighten on my shoulders. "Right?"

"Marsa..."

"What is it? Just tell me already."

He takes a deep breath. "We think it may be the bird you and Sosha saved."

"What? No. It can't be. It just can't." I push him to the side, shoving my way toward the offender. The bird is smashed and lifeless now, unable to do more damage, but it doesn't matter. It's already done too much.

And it's my fault. All my fault for insisting we help that stupid bird instead of letting Kaylyn eat it because it's most definitely that bird, a patch of white between its eyes.

"What have I done? Something so sweet shouldn't be allowed to turn evil."

"It shouldn't," Tavo says.

"It attacked the children. The children." It's

a struggle to keep my voice low.

Tavo rests a hand on my shoulder. "It's not your fault. You couldn't have known. None of us could."

"But I should have. Kaylyn didn't want to save it. I shouldn't have wanted to either."

"No, you were right trying to help it when it needed you."

I round on him. "And look where that got me. Just look what helping did. Granny will never see again. She's blind. Blind! Because of my choice."

I storm away, unable to keep my pent-up emotions stewing silently. Tavo lets me go into the dark world, alone without a torch. It doesn't take more than a few moments for the darkness to overcome me and press in with murky strength.

I whirl around, searching for the camp. Instead I find Tavo, patiently waiting nearby with a torch in his hand, lighting up my world.

"What have I done?" My words are soft this time, full of despairing anguish.

Without a word, he wraps his arms around me and pulls me in tight.

Chapter Twenty-Two

When I finally pull away I tell him, "Thank you."

"Anytime."

I give a partial smile, the closest I can come to the real thing right now.

"I mean it. Anytime you need anything, Marsa, I'm here."

It's these words I'm left to ponder on as we head back to camp. His strength, at least, is there for me when I can't seem to find my own.

The camp is quiet, settled for the night, somehow even more somber than before. I feel more somber than before. Tavo heads to his pack, but I wander the perimeter, wondering if I should check on Granny or Felix. I don't feel like I can face either of them right now. What's going to happen to them? Are we going to be able to get Felix back in time?

Kaylyn joins my pacing, and for a while, we're both silent. "Tavo and you were talking earlier."

I huff out a breath, wishing it would take all the guilt with it. "He told me about the bird."

"You couldn't have known."

"Exactly what he said. How bad will Granny's life be now that she's blind?" I dare ask.

"It's hard to know. I suspect it will be a difficult transition, but honestly, I have no idea."

I try to imagine what it'd be like to lose my sight but can't even fathom it. Difficult is an understatement.

"She's tough," Kaylyn says. "She'll be fine. She's already spouting off ways it may make her life better."

"It's Granny. She'll act tough, no matter what she really feels."

"Maybe. But it also means you probably don't need to worry as much as you think."

"Isn't that always the case?" She gives me a look, and I give her one right back.

"I think it'd be best to change the subject. So about Tavo…"

"What about him?" For some reason, my cheeks warm.

"I just found it interesting that you two were together."

"Why shouldn't we spend time together? He was letting me know about the stupid bird."

"So this doesn't change anything with Jorrin?"

"Jorrin?" Something twists inside me,

raking across my tender feelings. "Why would it?"

"Just curious." She glances into the darkness, but it's like she's not really seeing anything. Like she's looking into the distance so she doesn't have to look at me. Whatever it is, I'm not sure I want to explore it.

Before she can continue on the subject, I change it, though I should have changed it to something easier. "You know when we were talking about going into the forest?"

"What about it?"

This is so much harder than I thought it was going to be. "I should have told you then, and I didn't. I guess I wanted to be strong, like everyone else."

"Should have told me what?"

I take a steeling breath. "That I didn't think we should go in. That I didn't think it would have answers for us. I was scared to voice how I really felt, but I should have anyway."

After a moment, she says, "Please don't worry about it. We've all been scared this week."

"Do you think Felix is going to make it?" I ask, wishing she'll allay my fears.

"We'll get him home as soon as possible."

Which is really no answer at all. Except for maybe getting him home to say good-bye. I feel like sitting down right here on the outskirts of camp and sobbing. Instead, I numb myself as best I can.

"I suppose I should get to bed," Kaylyn says.

"Yeah. I suppose so, too." Maybe sleep will help me forget, at least for a little while.

Before she leaves, she says, "Next time I ask if we can eat a bird for dinner, the answer is yes."

"Only if you're doing the cooking," I reply, trying to keep the lighter mood she's striving for. In truth, it's just one more reminder of how badly I failed.

Chapter Twenty-Three

The morning starts off like any other in this dreadful place. That is, until Tavo rushes over.

"Felix has gotten worse."

I don't hesitate to run with him through the crowd toward Felix. I brace myself for the worst. "How bad?"

"They don't think he'll live much longer," he says between breaths.

It wasn't enough to brace myself. My heart drops, sinking far below the ground. Not Felix. I can't lose him, too. I just can't.

I fall to the ground, kneeling at his side across from Granny and Kaylyn, next to Jorrin. Even though I'm not touching him, I can feel the heat radiating off him. The wound itself is covered by a bandage, but streaks blacker than the darkest night peak out of it.

There is no hope for something like that. I don't even know what that is, but it's all I can focus on as silence fills the air around us. Those little black marks trailing out of the white bandage. Why do they have to be so harmful?

The world is silent around us as Felix slips further and further away from us. The villagers come, slowly at first, but more and more as time passes, yet they don't make a sound. The silence only makes things worse. It's not how Felix is. He's loud and happy and full of life. Not this deathwatch we're hovering over him.

I take hold of his hand as he shakes, giving him what little comfort I know how to give. Though with my own chest searing with pain, I don't know that I can give much. At least he seems too far gone to realize what's happening, though I wish I could have talked to him one last time. Why didn't I?

I grip both of his hands in mine and silently apologize for not talking to him more, until I realize I committed a worse sin. I shouldn't have let us go into that forest. If we had left with the villagers sooner, Felix's death wouldn't be on my hands.

With that last thought, Felix stops his subtle movements. Jorrin takes his pulse, and then shakes his head. Gone. Felix is no more because of me.

৯৽৶

An icy numbness spreads through me as I gather wood for the pyre. I don't know what to think or feel. Everything we strove for, all the work we've done, picks this moment to come crashing down. After losing my mom, I didn't think anyone else would be killed by the darkness. But I was wrong. Everything is controlled by the darkness.

I finish helping stack the wood together and step aside as Azleco, Foley, Jorrin, and Sosha carry Felix's body to the pyre and set him atop of it. Without the Aster and Astra here to lead the ceremony, we all look to Kaylyn.

Her jaw is so tense; I doubt she could open her mouth to speak. Who can blame her? All I want to do is cry out, not try to offer false comfort about loved ones watching over us.

I open my mouth anyway, taking away at least some of the weight Kaylyn has to carry because of my bad choice. "Felix was beloved by all. He truly cared about those around him, and he knew how to make others laugh, raising their spirits. As we continue this life with him watching us from above, may we remember him each time we find joy."

Too short, but it's all I have in me to give. The tears that have been threatening finally fall over the edge, down my cheeks, and into the dirt. Ground Felix should be walking on right now, along with Momma. The ache rumbles in my chest. I want to call out, a primal call of pain and defeat. Instead, I watch Jorrin light the pyre and send Felix to the stars, wondering how we are going to ever prevent more of our loved ones from leaving this world.

Chapter Twenty-Four

When we reach the canyon's end, I'm exhausted emotionally from losing Felix and physically because of the villagers. They are trying, and though some are used to a hard life, many are too old or young to be used to such a vigorous push.

"We're only a couple days from home," Sosha says.

Which would be good if it weren't still so dark.

"We should probably stop for the ni—erm, stop for a rest," Kaylyn says.

While I agree that the villagers need it, I wish we could press on as we need to do.

"Can anyone else feel their way out of this darkness?" Kaylyn asks.

It's a strange question. She's done just fine leading us and should be able to tell how much more space the darkness takes up. I haven't even tried to see for myself. My power is still snugly bundled inside, staying safely wrapped tight.

"I can." Jorrin's reply isn't unexpected. He's the second-in-command for good reason. "We should be able to make it out of here soon and then onto home. Unless you have another plan?"

"I can sense it, too," Azleco says.

"So we can all feel it." Or I'm sure I could if I tried. "How does this help?"

"It helps us know we're close," Kaylyn replies. "I don't have to lead you anymore. I think someone else should take that place."

My stomach drops. My mind goes blank.

"But you're our leader," Azleco says.

"I have been, but it's time for a change."

"Are you sure that's what you want?" Because it can't really be. Not with how she's been raised. With how she leads. With how she does everything. And not just because it's what she's supposed to do but because she's always loved doing it. Felt lost without it.

Her response is long in coming, quiet and thoughtful. "I admit it's definitely a change, for all of us, but I think it's needed."

A sort of numbness settles over me. There's more to this going on. I'm certain of it. And the way Jorrin stares her down, I'm certain he knows it, too. The only questions are: what is it, and why hasn't she shared it with us yet?

And why am I so concerned about it?

It doesn't take long for us to come to an agreement that Jorrin should take her place. He's the natural choice for the job, and though he's reluctant because of Kaylyn, he's willing on all other counts.

With him in charge, camp gets set up like usual, only he says things differently. Kaylyn's taking first watch. It'll be my turn just before it's time to set off for the day. Despite everything going on, it doesn't take long for the heavy drift of sleep to slow my thoughts. Only a noise stirs me.

It's Kaylyn. She's wandering the camp, moving between the sleeping people. What is she doing? She's supposed to be keeping watch. I let my gaze follow her until she's reaches Jorrin. Maybe she's just tired and needs to switch. She leans over him, hovering there. I wait for her to wake him, unable to take my gaze off the two of them.

Only the wait is so long, my eyes grow fuzzy and tired. I blink. When I open them again, Kaylyn is brushing a kiss on Jorrin's forehead. A strange iciness shudders through me. What is she doing? Why is she kissing him?

She hurries away from him without a glance in my direction. It was so swift, maybe I misinterpreted it.

Someone jostles my shoulder. My eyes open instantly, frantic energy pulsing through me. When I see whose face hovers above mine, a different sort of feeling pulses through me. A much better one, yet it's tainted with uncertainty. It's strange. Muddled.

"We need to talk," Jorrin says.

This isn't how I pictured finally having a conversation about us, but I jump up and hurry after him to the edge of camp. Kaylyn isn't on watch. Jorrin must have already relieved her of that duty. I didn't think he'd take the second watch with his new responsibilities, but then again, maybe it will give him time to think. Maybe that's what I saw before, Kaylyn telling him she'd need a break soon and the kiss on the forehead was just friendly?

At the edge of camp, he takes no time leaning closer. My stomach does odd little flips. Here it comes. Finally!

"Kaylyn is missing."

"What?" I'm almost shouting, but I can't help it. This was the last thing I expected.

He grabs my wrists, pulling me back toward him. I hadn't even realized I'd lurched back. "Shhh. I don't want to wake the others."

This is about her. I should have known. They've been so close together lately I've wondered—. Now isn't the time for it. Not if she's really gone. My stomach is still doing flips, but now they're raucous ones that leave me feeling sick. "What do you mean missing? Where could she have gone? Was there another attack we didn't hear?"

"No. You should be able to feel her with your Zophasken. She's heading back toward the village."

"What?" I realize I'm shouting again and work to quiet my voice. "Why could she possibly be heading back there?"

"I don't know, but I have to find out. If it's anything like the tree..."

No further explanation is needed. "What about the villagers?"

"Lead them for me? Please?"

I've never led anyone anywhere other than sometimes when I'd have a mission with one or two other Zophas. Is this really the best option? "Maybe one of the—?"

"I'll ask if I have to, but you're the best suited for this, Marsa. You've spent more time with your mother and Kaylyn than anyone else. You have the bravery and determination to do what needs to be done to get these people safe."

Something warms inside me, making me think his words are true, and not because he's Jorrin and I want to hear nice things from him. Because maybe, just maybe, he's right. Something in my gut says it'll be so, if only I'd stop giving in to my worries. "Do you really believe in me that much?"

He leans against the tree furthest away from me. "You are an excellent person, Marsa. Truly fit to be a Zophas. You run headlong into things, even when they frighten you. You do what's right. Yes, I believe you are the one to lead."

Not very swoon worthy, but just what I needed to hear. "Go get Kaylyn. Save her from herself."

"Does that mean you'll do it?"

"Yes, but you'd better hurry back."

"Thank you."

"A speedy return would be the best. Thanks," I say as he's already leaving, form fading as he moves into the fog-like darkness. I shouldn't yell. I'm not ready to wake the sleeping villagers I'm now in charge of.

I suppose that's it, then. I'm left to lead the crowd of people back to safety. I only wish I knew where safety was.

Chapter Twenty-Five

I don't bother waking anyone else to watch. With my hesitance to use my Zophasken, I probably should, but deep in my gut I feel things will be safe enough. We're not in the worst of the darkness anymore. At least the others said we were nearing the light of home. It should be good enough. Besides, it was supposed to be my watch soon anyway.

And the time I thought Jorrin was taking to think on how to handle his new position has suddenly fallen to me.

Why would Kaylyn just leave us like that? I can't fathom any reason she would. At least nothing that makes sense. Something probably did come up in her mind, though, whether reasonable or just plain self-sacrificial remains to be seen.

I have an urge to wake Tavo and talk with him about what's happened, but I can't bring myself to when he needs the sleep. Sosha, too.

These two are going to be my lifeline when they wake. Can't have them not at their best.

I find myself pacing the camp's boundary in the dark, alone and uncertain.

The day comes on too quickly, darker than it was the end of yesterday but still with enough light filtering through that we can see without aid the of torches. The others wake—just a few at first, then the entire camp seems to come to life, putting things away and making breakfast, and for the first morning, children's laughter rings through the camp. The ashy light must be good for them as well.

The other Zophas help each other and the villagers as needed. Tavo. What do I tell them? How do I tell them? Our leader gave up her position and then her designated substitute ran off after her. It's not an easy thing to think or say.

Sometimes I used to dream about what it'd be like to live in a perfect world where everyone only wanted goodness. Now it's here—well— things don't seem much different. Of course, there are no Malryx to fight. No lying or cheating or murdering to deal with, but it's not perfect. Even when one's intentions are wholly good, problems still arise. A perfect world isn't really so perfect.

"Hey, Marsa." Azleco comes up to me. "Have you seen Kaylyn or Jorrin? None of us have seen either one of them yet, and both their packs are missing."

I guess this means it's time. "Why don't you bring the Zophas over and we'll chat."

"That doesn't sound good." He frowns.

It most certainly isn't. Has Jorrin reached her yet? Are they safe? Are they headed back to us? To me? "Everything will be fine."

As Azleco leaves to get the others, I wonder how often Kaylyn had to force a confidence she didn't feel. It almost feels bad, but it's what they need to hear. It's good for us all to focus on the positive. Maybe getting that through to them will help me, too.

It doesn't take them nearly long enough to gather. The villagers keep an eye on us but don't act as if they think anything is wrong, going on with making breakfast and packing up camp. How am I supposed to be responsible for all of them? What am I even going to tell them? If I had more time, maybe I could come up with something useful, though I did have a large chunk of the night to think on it. The thought makes me yawn.

"Too early for you?" Tavo teases.

"It's always too early for her," Sosha says with a chuckle.

A typical comeback that would tease them back never rises to my lips. The weight placed on me is too great for any of that. Since nothing else comes to mind, I plunge ahead.

"So you've all noticed Kaylyn and Jorrin are missing." As they nod, I can't help but think that wasn't the smoothest of starts. "They

210

are..." Missing. Possibly never returning. Going back to the darkness. Alone together. Wait, why does that matter? And I need to think of something. The other Zophas all stare at me. "... trying to figure some things out. Jorrin asked me to help him while they're gone." A range of emotions displays about what I've been trying to deal with ever since Jorrin woke me. Confusion. Worry. Panic.

"We're sure you'll make an excellent leader until they get back," Tavo says.

I smile my thanks even if the sentiment doesn't reach my heart. The others chime in their agreement with Tavo but so quickly we're back to being silent. Kaylyn would fill this type of silence with orders.

I'm not her. I could never fill her shoes. There was a reason the Aster and Astra choose her instead of me even though my mother was the leader.

"What should we tell the villagers?" Sosha asks.

"Just what I told you." Much greater confidence than I actually feel fills my words. "They should know Kaylyn and Jorrin enough by now to understand they're doing what's best. Let's help the villagers pack up for the day. I want to put us as close to home as possible before Kaylyn and Jorrin return. Wouldn't they be pleased if we managed to get everyone there before their return?" I hope they won't be so lost in the darkness that they can't find us.

The words seem to give the Zophas what they need. They bounce to their work, or at least get to it with a quicker, more certain step than before. Though I help as I usually do, I'm often stopped to answer a question about minor details. Things I didn't even know Kaylyn was handling. It's not as hard as I thought it would be, though. Whatever my response, they seem happy enough to follow.

As everyone gets packed up and ready to head out, I realize a slight flaw in my leading. I haven't a clue where to lead everyone to. I step off to the side and look at the group like I'm making certain everything's ready to go. Really, though, I'm preparing myself to do what I haven't done since before we reached the darkness.

Release my Zophasken into the world.

Its warmth is centered in me, protecting my core as always. I focus on that, on its goodness. Its protection, even when things are dark all around. Even if it doesn't like how the darkness feels, it will do what needs done to save these people. And me.

I slowly push its power out. It moves more quickly than I remember, its strength growing since I last used it. I rein it in, keeping a tighter hold on it. No sense scaring it off with a flash into the dark world all at once. I let it yawn and stretch, creeping its way past my immediate being. There's no darkness right away, but it's only a few feet from me. It doesn't take long to feel the oily slime brush against my power. Both my power and I shiver away.

I plant myself to the ground, steeling my power. This isn't the time to shirk. It needs to be taken care of because I can't stay in this place any longer. I shove my power out this time, forcing it into the darkness it cringes away from.

"I was thinking," Azleco says, startling me. When did he sneak up? "You're really good working with the people. I know you're in charge now, so I'm willing to do whatever you want, but if you'd like, I can lead us out. That way you can focus on the people instead of finding the light through the darkness."

I want to yank him into a hug. "How thoughtful. Thanks, Azleco. I think I may just take you up on that offer. I really do enjoy being with them."

"Whatever you want."

I want to declare him my favorite person ever. "Why don't we go ahead and gather everyone? I think they're ready."

"Of course."

Together, we walk toward the villagers. Something is a little different, though I can't figure out quite what. It presses on me. Weighty. Caving in my chest. Pounding on my thoughts. I should talk to Kaylyn when I see her again, or Tavo. Or someone? Anyone? But what would I say?

Silly thoughts. I'm sure I can talk to Kaylyn. It's just the pressure of leading. It's different. Nothing like I'm used to. I didn't know she carried this type of weight inside, but it makes sense now that I think about it.

"Are you doing okay?" Tavo asks.

I smile at him. "Better now. Just trying to get used to being a leader. I'm not sure I'm any good at it."

"Of course you are."

I roll my eyes at him.

"I mean it. Like when you've led me before on small missions. Or when the bird attacked. You didn't sit back and wait for someone to tell you what to do. As soon as you knew what was needed, you followed through and yelled at the rest of us to do so as well. It's not the title that makes you a leader. It's what's inside you, and you've already got what it takes."

My cheeks heat. His words continue to warm me as we join the others. The Zophas spare no thought or concern to Azleco's leading us toward home. No thought to my mingling with the villagers and helping whoever needs anything. It's as if it was supposed to be this way. I still call out time for breaks just before it seems like one is needed, and unfortunately, tell them we need to stop for the night.

Everyone listens as if I was—well, not Kaylyn, but as if I were a leader. My first day is successful despite my not actually showing the way. Maybe Tavo's right. Maybe there's more inside me than I think there is. I still can't help but look behind us, wondering if Kaylyn and

Jorrin will be here soon. What could possibly be keeping them?

Chapter Twenty-Six

The next day, there's still no sign of them. Today we'll reach home. Azleco assured me of that. There's sweetness to the thought, but it's muddied by two very horrid things. The darkness hasn't left. It's stretched out before us and over what must be home. It's not black encased, more like a gray tinge to the air. A light gray, but still gray.

Nature's evil is invading my home, and there's nothing we can do about it. There's no denying that, no matter how much I try.

The worst thing, though, is that Kaylyn and Jorrin still haven't joined us. Are they lost? Are they injured? Are they still alive? Or could it be they've abandoned us? It's wrong to think such thoughts, but I can't help it. What could possibly be keeping them from joining us?

I put on a brave face for the others, and they seem to accept it. But what will the Aster and Astra say when I show up without them? I feel as if I'm failing as a leader, leaving two of our best behind. But there's no other way to take the villagers back, and I can't leave them. Enough of us are gone already. There's so few of us left to protect them without another person abandoning them.

"Today's the day," I tell each villager as I help them along. "We'll reach the village today, even if it means walking past dark."

It's unlikely we'll need to since the words put an eager step in their pace. Not the frantic hurry we first started with on this journey, but with a bounce of hope.

I say the same to Tavo after I've helped all the villagers who need it at the moment. It doesn't give him the same bounce, though.

He lowers his voice. "How far is this darkness going to spread?"

"I don't know." My throat tightens. I lower my voice even more than his. "I don't think we're going to have much of a home left soon."

His lips tighten like I just confirmed his fears; nothing further shows of his worries, though. He moves closer to me as we both keep an eye on the villagers, ready to help should the need arise. When he finally speaks again, it's in an unexpected direction.

"About the lying game..." Tavo hesitates.

My thoughts immediately fly back to it, even though it seems so long ago. Tavo, Sosha, and I around the campfire with Felix. Just the thought of him makes my heart ache. If only we'd know how long we had left with him. At least some of our last days had moments of joy.

I realize my thoughts have been wandering, and Tavo still hasn't finished his sentence. "What about it?"

"Which one was the lie?"

Am I happy? Or do I miss the Malryx?

I don't know.

⊱⊰

Tavo turns behind us suddenly.

"What is it?" I draw my sword, fearing the worst. What could be attacking us now?

I barely have time to register his quizzical glance at my sword before Jorrin and Kaylyn burst through the trees.

The tight cord binding my chest since Kaylyn and Jorrin's departure snaps apart. They're alive! And almost... glowing? Why would they be glowing?

It's then I realize why Tavo gave me such a strange glance. Because I should have known it was them. I should have felt them with my Zophasken. At least it's the end of the journey before someone realized I was keeping it tucked where it would be safe. I'll let it out if I have to, but what good would it do now?

"You're back!" says Azleco.

The joyful shout sends a ripple through the villagers, like a bonfire lighting the night with its waves. They are back. And safe.

"There isn't time to tarry," Kaylyn shouts before they even reach us.

"Keep moving," Jorrin says. "We're not stopping again until we reach home."

It doesn't have to be said twice. The villagers turn back toward Azleco, who presses us forward, faster than ever. I grab a young girl, perhaps two years old, and lift her to my back as we hurry forward. Not much farther compared to how far we've come.

I alternate children as we walk. Most keep up their tireless energy, but it's clear the carrying helps. There's only so fast their little legs can go and only so much carrying their parents can handle. I often find an elderly person to walk next to, giving them my arm to hold on to so they can move along. Frustration simmers in the eyes of some. They know they're slowing us down, and they don't like it, but they're doing the best they can. We all are.

Granny manages as if she's neither old nor blind. Occasionally she pauses for just a moment, such a small moment, but it makes me wonder if this is all harder on her than she's trying to make it out to be. Whenever I try to help her, she shoos me off to someone else. I can only hope the fast pace isn't too difficult on her frail, still-healing body.

A time happens where all the kids seem to be moving fast enough and no one needs help. I move to Kaylyn's side.

"What happened?"

"I thought there was something that might help with the darkness, but it didn't." The sparkle that's been in her eyes since her return dims. Isn't that backward? I'm more confused than ever.

"What did you try?"

She shakes her head but doesn't say anything, lips forming a thin line.

"Did something else happen?" I persist. "I'm getting this odd feeling from you. A strange mix of happy and sad."

She rubs the hilt of her sword with her thumb. "We should focus on getting the villagers home."

The dismissal stings. What happened to my best friend? Why won't she talk to me? I edge away from her, pretending to check on the back of the group. Tavo sees me and meets me there.

"Any news?"

"I think she just brushed me off."

His raises his brow. At least I'm not the only one surprised by her behavior. "Jorrin's not saying anything either."

"I don't know if that's comforting or worse."

"Maybe they're just trying to concentrate on getting us home. Or they want to talk to the Aster and Astra before us."

"It wouldn't be the first time." Then again, it'd be the first time they needed to do so that they didn't just say so. The sting follows through the rest of the journey.

We're nearing home. I can feel it in my bones. I can also feel it in my legs and shoulders. My shoulders especially ache from the constant carrying of little ones, but I'd like to think it made a difference. We'll make it before nightfall. The sting from Kaylyn's dismissal is still the worst, though.

It's still the ashy gray outside. Each day, as we've walked it's gotten a little brighter, but today... Today it feels and looks a little duller. Like the movement of the clouds isn't just thinning out like it was before we went to the village, but it's spreading more rapidly. How much of the world will it cover? And how will it affect our lives? It's difficult to say for certain, but I do know that the new conditions it's created aren't livable by humans. At least not in long-term survival with food and shelter.

The village is in disarray as we arrive. People are running everywhere, hurrying to pack things together. It looks like our frantic pace to get here is going to be met by our people frantically leaving. Not a surprise. Just what I expected, but still, it hurts. I'm tired of being on the run. Tired of fighting something that can't be fought. And tired of keeping my power safe inside.

Kaylyn tells Azleco to lead the villagers to a clearing on the far side of the village, where they'll all fit, and then she hurries with Jorrin toward the center of the village. The people seem fine, like they'll be all right without me for a time. I hurry after Kaylyn and Jorrin, not to be left in the dark if I can help it.

We have to find out how to not only take care of ourselves but to take care of the villagers, and I want to know what Kaylyn is keeping from me. The Aster and Astra are waiting for us, like two lonely mountain peaks.

"What have you learned?" the Astra asks the moment we are before them.

Jorrin and Kaylyn exchange some type of silent communication. I want to speak up, to tell them what's happened and demand answers from the two of them, but he's supposed to be in charge, and she really is.

After a moment, Kaylyn says, "We think nature is changing because there are no more Malryx. Nature is trying to balance out their loss."

The faces of our leaders mirror the horror in my own heart. At least I've had time to deal with it, even if I don't understand it.

Mirgen heads toward us, and the Aster waves her off. "Not now," he chokes out. "We will speak with you all soon."

Mirgen wavers, seemingly unsure of what to do, but then follows the order, hurrying back toward where everyone is gathering. The fact the Aster is turning someone away washes me in cold chills. They never turn anyone away. Never.

"Balance," the Aster says. "Could it be?"

"All these years, we thought..." The Astra

trails off.

It seems as if they've forgotten us. Another mark that things are seriously, seriously wrong. I'd always looked up to them, thought them capable of everything, of always guiding and directing us, but in this one moment, it all shatters. They are just as fallible as us, even if their intentions are wholly good.

"What have we done? What madness have we pushed this world to?" The Aster staggers and might have fallen if Jorrin didn't move to his side to steady him.

"We did what we thought was best," the Astra replies, seemingly calm, but her hands are white from gripping each other. "We couldn't have known this would happen. We've never been able to rid the world of evil people before. Now we know we can't rid the world of evil at all."

The Aster's lips thin. "But the balance. We never even considered the balance needed for life."

After a moment of silence, Kaylyn says, "We think there might be a way to undo that." She points at the darkening clouds coming closer.

"What is it, my child?" The Aster's voice is riddled with urgency.

"We need to bring the Malryx back."

But—*What*?

All those Malryx I helped kill were for nothing. No, not just nothing—now we're supposed to bring them back somehow? I want to laugh so hard my chest aches with repressing it. It's too much. I should have realized, but I would have never dreamed it. Is this what Kaylyn was hiding from me?

When the Astra finally speaks, it's a struggle for me to listen to her. "It would stand to reason they would need to be brought back. You have more experience with them than we do. What do you propose?"

Kaylyn's reply is so faint, I have to strain to hear her. "I tried to become Malryx but failed."

"You did what?" The words rage from me before I can stop them. "What would we do without either of you?"

"You would survive, like you always do," Kaylyn says.

My anger still burns but cooler. This is what she hid from me. That she tried to leave me. Become someone I would have to hunt down. Not to kill anymore, apparently, but to hunt down and imprison. Forever.

But she may have a valid point about me surviving without her, even if I don't want to hear it. I did much better than I expected leading the villagers then. I survived and coped. Even when I left the Zophas earlier than Kaylyn did, I managed without her. But those were little things. Times when we would always see one another again. If she succeeded, our next meeting wouldn't be a happy one. We couldn't be friends.

"Marsa, you know you're like a sister to me. No one means more to me, and I mean no one. That doesn't change the fact that I have to do what's right, what's needed, even if it makes things hard for us."

"By hard you mean impossible."

"Maybe so."

"There is no maybe." My anger is all burned out. Even when she's trying to become bad, she's good. Looking out for the best of everyone, even when it means something hard for us. I couldn't do the same. I can't' help it.

I hug Kaylyn, wrapping my arms around her tight. "I'm so relieved you didn't change." I sob out.

"Me too." Her voice is coated in tears too.

When we pull apart, Jorrin holds a handkerchief toward us. I pull out my own and let Kaylyn take his. Once we're somewhat reassembled, I realize this display took place in front of the Aster and Astra, and a blush follows. Even if they're just people, it was rather dramatic and personal.

"As glad as I am," Kaylyn says, giving me a meaningful look. "It doesn't change the fact that we still need to fix this."

"Is there any way?" the Aster says.

"We need to find someone to turn." Kaylyn's words are stern, and though I know it's needed, ice pricks my heart.

"And we need to do it without telling them," Jorrin says. "If they know, it could change their motives for trying to turn, which will prevent them from being able to."

"And we need to do it quickly."

Oh, stars! How can we do this to someone? How can we not?

Kaylyn continues, "Do either of you know anyone in the village who may be on the brink? People questioning whether what we do is good?"

"I know of no one," the Astra says.

"None of the villagers would turn," the Aster says. "I know of nobody that would turn, except maybe the Zophas." Another sob chokes me. He seems to know how hard this must be for us to hear, his words quiet and soft. "Being around evil so much has a way of letting it sneak into you, even if you think you're only fighting against it.

"If we turn our friends evil..." Jorrin's words are heavy with repressed emotion.

"Will it make us evil?" Kaylyn finishes his thought.

When did they become so in tune with each other?

It doesn't matter now. "We'll forever have guilt over it whether it turns us evil or not."

"After all you three have done? You won't turn evil," the Astra says. "If anything, you'd turn if you didn't try. If you gave into your own selfish desire to keep your friends at all cost."

Maybe I'm evil. I want to keep them. Nothing inside me feels different, though. I don't think I'm evil, despite having this desire. It's good to want to take care of our friends and loved ones, even if it means not wanting them to turn evil.

"We must attend the people," the Aster says. "This is a choice you three alone will know how to handle best. If there is something you need, please let us know."

"We will," Kaylyn says.

It's true she will never really leave us, despite her words.

She starts to bow, but the Astra immediately stops her. "No, my child. It is we who should be bowing to you. Begging for your forgiveness for being so blinded by our desire to thwart evil we lost sight of the need for balance."

"If we survive," the Aster adds, "there will be much for us to atone for."

And then they bow, giving us the full amount of respect usually reserved for them. It leaves a numbing sort of surprise in me as they hurry off toward Mirgen who's waiting for them.

"We need to get on this," I say as soon as I come to my senses, the words making me sick.

"Who can we do it to, though?" Kaylyn asks.

"One of the Zophas we left in the village or someone we took with us?" Jorrin replies.

They discuss a few options, but the thought just makes me sick. I can't even focus on what they're saying. On what we're trying to accomplish. We're like animals, turning on one another for survival. No, not animals. Malryx. Evil.

Still, they don't choose anyone. We're all trying to avoid actually making a decision.

"What about Tavo?" Kaylyn says.

"No!" The word burns my throat. Not him. We can't do this to Tavo. My words have shocked them. They've shocked me. "I mean, I'm just not sure about him turning..." I can't even finish the thought.

"Maybe he could." Jorrin looks like he wants to do anything but reply, even if the thought has merit. "He's good but sometimes troubled. He could be the answer."

No. Not Tavo. Anyone but him. It may be the right suggestion, but I just can't.

"Has he ever said anything to either of you?" Kaylyn asks me. She's the calmest of us all right now, holding everything together. Or maybe it really doesn't bother her. After all, she's trying to do what's best for everyone else. Everyone else over one person.

"No," I choke out. "But sometimes he seems almost..."

"Bitter?" Kaylyn says what I can't.

"Yes," Jorrin says. "I think there may be a chance with him. Stars save us."

Yes indeed. Stars save us all, but I think it's much too late for that.

Chapter Twenty-Seven

"How are we going to do this?" Jorrin says.

When Kaylyn stays silent, I say, "If it's all right, I think I'd prefer to try to force the change at our old Zophas home. We'll either succeed or have to try with one of the other Zophas. If none of it works, I think I'd rather face the end there."

It's the best I can get under the circumstances. It's finally time to go to my real home.

"I would prefer that as well." Kalyn's reply is soft. "Besides, if nature is trying to balance things out, it has to stop at some point. If the others leave now, hopefully they'll be able to stay ahead of the spread until they find a place that will remain unaffected by the taint."

"Maybe we should just leave the taint, then." The words just slip from me.

Kaylyn and Jorrin stare at me as if I've gone as crazy as the enraged sheep and bird.

"It could work." I press on, my voice small.

"Or it could devour all life for hundreds of more miles," Kaylyn says. "Make it impossible for us to live. Who knows? Maybe it will become a fight of nature trying to balance out the mess we've created that causes such problems that all of humanity is destroyed."

I nod, though I still wish it would work. It's a better plan than trying to turn Tavo.

"I'll go tell the Astra and Aster so they can plan accordingly," Jorrin says.

He and Kaylyn exchange a glance that holds more meaning in it than I want to think on. I hurry to look away. Now isn't the time to worry over silly feelings.

As soon as he's gone, Kaylyn says, "Are you going to be all right? Helping us try to turn Tavo?"

No. Never. "How can we change anyone? I know the consequences if we don't, but it's too horrid to even contemplate."

"I know, Marsa. I know," she says, voice small. "I'm sorry I got us into this."

"You didn't get us into this." Though she did help, but that's not what she needs to hear right now. "It's been a goal my mother worked toward her entire life. Many people have worked on it. The Astra and Aster didn't just support it but helped guide it along. It's not your fault."

"But I killed the last one. Nature didn't seem to explode with evil until I put it in motion."

"You were doing what you thought was best."

"Is what we're doing now what seems best? What if it's wrong? What if we only make things worse?"

I've never heard such misgivings from her. Such doubt. "I only know things will be even worse within ourselves if we don't try."

"So maybe we shouldn't. Maybe we should stop trying. Maybe then I could turn evil and not have to force someone else. Just like the Astra suspects."

"I know you. Have known you our whole lives. Would you really be giving up, or would you be giving up so you would turn?"

She sighs. "To turn, of course, which would make me not turn. I just hate this. Hate having to turn someone. This should never have to be. If anyone should go, it should be me." By the time she finishes, she's almost yelling.

The passion from her surprises me. Maybe she does feel more about it than she's been showing. "I know. I feel the same way."

We grip each other in a tight hug then and let the fears and worries and sadness of what must be done force our grips tight. I don't want to let her go. Don't want to face what's going to happen. But the sky is growing even darker.

We gather together any Zophas who are willing to fight to the end with us, and the rest go with the Aster and Astra. All those who traveled to the village join us, as do a few others.

Our first duty is to help see everyone off on their journey. There's more than enough time to see if our plan will succeed or fail, but who knows how long they'll need to get far enough away should it come to the worst?

As they are walking away, Granny is off to the side, unmoving, cane in hand. I go to her. "Would you like me to find someone to guide you?"

"I've been guiding myself just fine this whole time, thank you very much," she snaps, but it's quickly followed by a long, tired sigh. "I'm just done with the journeying. I think I'll stay here and let nature take me."

"You can't!"

"It's no different than what you're doing."

"We're trying to fix it."

Though I know she can't see, she gives me a look that says she *can* see through me, deep inside my soul.

I don't have the willpower to fight her. "You're welcome to join us. It's quite a hike up the mountain, though, and I know you want to rest."

"Nonsense." She straightens like she was never really tired in the first place. "No mountain has beaten me yet."

And I swear if this one does, I'll carry her up, even if I have to listen to her complain about it the entire way. Something about her coming soothes me. Her presence may not be vital for

232

turning Tavo, but it's vital for my sanity.

The climb up the mountain is harder than ever. Not physically. It's almost too easy of a climb, even for Granny, but the dark clouds continue rolling in overhead, darkening our way. My thoughts darken as well as Tavo walks close by my side. I want to reach out to him. To grab his hand. To hold on tight. But I can't do that to him now. Not with what we're about to do.

So I make myself just walk between Granny and Tavo, pointing out a rock or dip in the path to Granny, but otherwise remaining silent. When we reach the top and go to the fire pit by our old home, the valley below is a mix of shadow and light. How much time will it take for the darkness to finish the job?

We start a fire and gather around it. I keep Granny and Tavo both close, as if somehow that will protect both them and me from what's to come. When Jorrin speaks, I want to slap my hand over his mouth.

"What a waste our lives have been. We should have been taking it easy instead of fighting the Malryx."

The others look nervous, not making eye contact with him. If I didn't know his plan, I'd think he'd suddenly gone mad. This doesn't seem like a way to get just Tavo, it's more like he's trying to push any of them. Though I'm grateful, I still inch closer to Tavo.

"Youth should be for playing, and instead they made us waste it," Jorrin continues.

Granny grunts.

"What's your problem, old woman?" Jorrin asks.

I jump to my feet. "What's wrong with you? You can't treat her like that!"

Jorrin glances up at the sky, like he's wishing the stars were there to help give him patience. I hurry and sit down, trying to tell myself to let him goad the others. I grab hold of Granny's hand and give it a squeeze. She squeezes back, giving me a smirk. If I didn't know better, I'd think she was in on the plan, too.

"Maybe," Kaylyn says. "But it doesn't change the fact that we've wasted our lives. To think we could have been enjoying each other's company more if it weren't for all this mess."

"It very well could be that we've wasted our lives," Tavo says.

I glance at him, wondering exactly what his thought process is right now. What goes through his mind? But as the others talk about what Kaylyn and Jorrin say, Tavo just looks at me, and I at him. He won't change. Nothing we can do will fix that. He may have faults, but he's too good for that. We're all too invested in the goodness of our people to change that. What an epic fail.

"Maybe we should all leave," Sosha says.

"Why is that?" I ask her.

"I think we're all going to die up here."

But we'd all die down there as well. At

least here, we have a type of peace.

Chapter Twenty-Eight

I sit next to Tavo, staring at the flames. They grow brighter as the sky grows darker, just like my guilt. Why would I ever agree to try to change Tavo? There are no words to say to take back what we just put him through. What I put him through.

Kaylyn and Jorrin are off to the side of the fire, talking. Again. It's all they ever seem to want to do anymore—be together. Not that I can blame them for leaving me out of the conversation. I'm so contrary lately. I've been against every decision made since this whole debacle started. They don't need something else like that, but the way they both seem to lean toward each other like their very thoughts are intertwining makes the pain around my chest tighten.

Suddenly, they aren't just leaning toward each other, but Kaylyn is actually leaning on him, her head hidden against his neck. The pain sharpens. As dark as it's getting, they probably think we can't see. That they're far enough from the fire they're immune from its light. No wonder they were always running off together. They are together.

I jump to my feet.

"What's wrong?" Tavo hurries to my side, offering his help even though I betrayed him. He must see what I'm staring at because he says, "Oh," before plopping back down.

Part of me longs to talk to him, to stay and try to fix this, but I don't know what to say. Tavo is my good friend who seems hurt by their actions as well, but Kaylyn is my best friend. She should have at least had the decency to tell me.

Instead of facing something I can't fix, I march over to the embracing couple. "Isn't this a cozy picture?"

Kaylyn jumps and faces me, guilt marring the glow she got from snuggling up to Jorrin. The man I told her I was going to marry.

"The darkness seems to be growing," I say. "The others would probably like you to say something."

I turn and leave without another word, the pain in my chest feeling like my sister just ripped out my heart.

The sky seems to react to my pain, the darkness intensifying to a point worse than being back in the forest. The air isn't just thick with darkness, it's heavy. Lightning strikes, a flash of bright purple like I've never seen, followed by a boom of thunder so strong it pulses my body.

For a moment no one moves or speaks. I can still feel the force of thunder raging through me. Or is it my anger at Kaylyn's betrayal? It's not that she's with Jorrin that hurts. It's that she's done so without talking to me.

"Maybe we should go," Tavo says.

Despite our telling them we wouldn't be leaving this place, the others look like they agree with him. I agree with him. Nature acting like this could cause a very painful death, yet something about it doesn't feel quite as scary as before. My power doesn't press in on itself like before but comfortably settles within.

I suppose when one is betrayed by their best friend, other things don't seem as bad.

"I'm tired of running," Kaylyn says.

She sits a ways from the fire, still close to the cave, pulling Jorrin to sit down by her. But that's not all. Jorrin doesn't just sit by her, rather he is pressed against her side, his gaze on her bright, even with the fire so far and the darkness closing in. He never looked at me like that.

Kaylyn rests her head on his shoulder, clinging on to him like an infatuated girl. The back of my foot bumps against a rock. When did I start moving backward?

Tavo is close at my side as Kaylyn and Jorrin gaze at each other in a way that makes me want to look away. But I can't. My gaze is locked on their love. A love that doesn't look new or shy at all, but as though it's been hidden from us for a long time. How long has their betrayal been going on and we didn't know? I didn't know?

"What are you two doing?" Tavo asks. "We've got to get out of here."

"I'm tired of running and fighting. You can leave if you want, but we're staying." Her gaze turns to Tavo briefly but is quickly back on Jorrin with a sort of devoted expression usually reserved for newlyweds. I can't look away from it. My vision is locked on their display, thoughts churning with a sort of numbness about their betrayal.

Suddenly they're kissing. Not a sweet, quick peck, but something heated with passion, and it doesn't end there. Kaylyn curls up on his lap so she can have better access to his lips. In front of us all. In front of me. Without ever saying a word about how she felt about it. My best friend didn't even have the courage to tell me the truth.

It's going to turn her evil.

Suddenly they're not just kissing, but whispering to each other, brushing their noses together, sharing some deep emotion. Every action feels like shards of ice stabbing into my soul.

"What are you two little love birds whispering about? Something you'd like to share with us? Something you'd like to tell your *friends?*" Because if not, they'll turn for sure, though it may already be too late. You don't hide a relationship like this from your friends without consequences.

Without turning to look at me, Kaylyn says, "I suppose it's time to tell you. Jorrin and I are in love."

Lightening brightens the sky at her announcement, coating the scene in its eerie purple light while bits of gray float through the air. It's hard to try to process what the gray stuff could be when the torment inside me is so severe.

The roar of the wind grows, smashing the gray bits. I realize it's ash from the volcano, everywhere. It's been thousands of years since it erupted, but now it feels like the perfect time to make its fury known. Kaylyn, our leader, the chosen one, is going evil, and will take Jorrin with her.

"You don't mind?" she yells at me over the roar.

I shrug, unsure what I can stay to stop this. My loss over Jorrin hurts, but I realize now that I never really had him. He was always kind but nothing more. But she knew how I felt. She knew she was going behind my back. There's nothing I can say that will fix this. Nothing I can say that will save her. Still, I can try.

"You don't have to do this," I say.

Instead of helping, she condemns herself further. "Oh, but I do. I've always wanted to be with him."

This is worse. Though, I figured it by the way they gazed at each other, and it was hinted at the way they were always alone together. But admitting it, and saying she purposefully went behind my back without telling me what was going on, dooms her to evil.

"I saw you, that night you left us all alone in the forest. You kissed him before you left, the man I love, but you didn't even look my way." My heart feels like it's ripping to shreds.

"He was the one I didn't want to leave."

Maybe there's something I can say to help. Something I can say to save a sister. "I saw the way he looked at you. What he said about not loving me was the truth, but I didn't know how you felt. I thought the kiss was just friendship mixed with the tension of the moment. I kept waiting for you to talk to me about it. For you to come to me."

It's now she can redeem herself. Be the Kaylyn I know. I don't care if it destroys the world. Someone else can fall and save us in time, but not her. Not Kaylyn.

"I did tell your mom all about it. It was easy to talk to her, and she agreed. She thought I'd be better for him anyway."

My heart drops. Momma? She talked to Mom but not me? And my mom agreed with her, that I wouldn't be any good for Jorrin?

I push the thought away—shove it with all my might. This can be sorted out later. Right now, I need to save her. Save her from these thoughts and actions that will put her on a path she doesn't belong on.

Before I can say a word, she continues. "In fact, that's what I was doing when I should have been out helping her defeat Morphrac. I was daydreaming about how Jorrin and I would be able to be together soon. I knew my time fighting was almost over, and there would be nothing left to stop us. Guess I should have been helping your mother instead."

No. No, she didn't. She couldn't.

"Even with her dying breath, Showna wanted to help me, though I failed her by my daydreaming." Kaylyn smiles. Cold. Hard. Cruel. She's turned. "Still, she always did love me best."

I realize then what it's come down to. I don't want to save her. I want her to pay for what she's done. For costing Mom's life. For leading us all through hell on a fool's errand she created.

"You don't know what you've done." Despite the thunder and lightning, my words are strong, enough to crash into her.

"Your mooning over a boy caused Showna to die?" Tavo's words burn like my own anger. Sosha is at our side, staring down Kaylyn and Jorrin.

They're not who I thought they were. Good is not what I thought it was. All my life I thought good was right, but now I see what it really brings. Selfishness that caused my mother to die and my best friend to turn into a twisted person.

Rage screams out of me, filling the valley with my fury. The storm seems like nothing compared to the tempest unleashing within me.

"I will never forgive you, Kaylyn. Never." The words feel like poison in my mouth. She should never have caused such feelings. The darkness inside me. The darkness...

For a moment, I waver, and time seems to slow. Darkness in me. I reach out my power, not Zophasken any longer, but rich Malkine, evil power, to Tavo and Sosha. They're filled with it, too. We're all the same. Not evil, but powerful. Holding the strength to do what needs doing.

The storm is cooling, almost like it's cooling into us. Could Kaylyn have—? No. Whatever she's done is done, and I can't ever think on it again.

Time speeds up again, my surroundings coming into hyper-clear focus. "You won't see vengeance coming until it's blasted you apart."

While the others stand there stunned, I grab my pack, mindful of all the things we're going to need. There's nothing we can leave behind. Tavo and Sosha mimic my movements, grabbing their own packs and snatching a few of the others as we leave. We go away from the others as fast as we can run. Away from the Zophas we once were but who we'll now fight against.

The Aster and Astra were right. Those closer to the Malryx are more apt to become one. No wonder others turned from the Zophas. The power coursing through me is nothing like the Zophasken. It's dark and strong, filling me with the potential to do what needs done.

Zophas are not what I thought they were. They're people who claim to be good but follow their own skewed selfish desires. My sole purpose now is to rid the world of their slanted views of goodness.

Chapter Twenty-Nine

I let myself think on what Kaylyn did now. On the truth of what she did. She turned me, for the sake of saving everyone from the growing threat nature had become. And now, she'll have to save them from me, only this time, there will be no killing the Malryx. She knows better than that. They all do.

Even though I understand what she did, it doesn't change me back. If I would have let myself think on it before, when I first changed, maybe things would be different. But now, in the depths of my heart, I don't even want to change. I don't want to be a Zophas. Anyone who could claim such slanted views is not filled with goodness, but cunning. I don't know how I lived all those years without seeing their ploy. Not only that, but how I lived all those years as one of them. I shudder. At least I've come to see the truth.

We Malryx only kill those who try to kill

us, who stand in the way of freedom and life, and of how we want to live and be.

"Are you going now?" Tavo asks.

"We could use more recruits. I'm sure I can find a few. Or at least get us some food until there's somewhere safe for us to be." And of course, by "get us some food" I mean steal it. The Zophas would never let us have any. For all their talk of goodness, they'd rather let us starve than help us in our time of need. So I have to do what I must to protect those who are closer to me than family.

"That's not all though, is it?"

"I don't know what you mean." I tie up my pack, keeping my fingers busy and my gaze down.

"You're going to see her."

I finally look up at him, head held high. "Maybe I am."

"Just be careful."

And then he kisses me. His lips on mine, and mine on his, flowing together like we aren't sure when we're going to see each other again, because we really don't know. She won't kill me if she sees me, but that doesn't mean she won't try to capture me.

He pulls me closer to him, keeping me warm with our connection. I don't know how I never saw this before. I don't know why I let some idea of Jorrin shroud what really mattered. A relationship with a sister who can't care for anyone, who is only concerned with her people as a whole and not individuals.

Tavo though... he understands. As does Sosha, and the other followers we gained. Our group is important, yes, but so are our individual wants and needs. I won't be swayed again.

"I'll see you soon," he says.

"Not soon enough." I give him another kiss, fierce and hard, and hurry off.

The way the land moves beneath my feet is familiar. Now that I'm not just back in shape, but stronger than ever, it's easy again. Though my time helping in the gardens with the herbs was useful in helping me set up a place for my people to live, it didn't offer the same vigor this does.

Something in me twinges as the valley comes into view. And the mountain. The tallest around. The highest, like the Zophas think of themselves. Above us all, so high, they tell us what we have to do. Not in so many words, of course, but the effect is the same. It's time to change that.

And what if we turned or killed them all like they did to the other Malryx? If nature turned against them to balance itself out, would it give us only good things if we got rid of them all? Would it become a paradise to live in?

Things to think on...

I stretch out my Malkine across the world. Funny how much easier it is now than it ever was when I was a Zophas. There's no movement across it yet, no one nearby, but I should come across someone. Of course I'm not looking for someone in general, I'm looking for her.

Though I didn't come all this way without getting something else from it as well.

There she is, bright like I expected, grating against my power with her superiority shining out of her. She's alone, or at least alone enough. No one is close enough to get in the way of my plans for her.

I skirt closer, somewhere that has a clear getaway, just in case, though I really don't think it's needed. Assuming things go as I expect.

Once she's close, I walk slowly toward her just to keep moving, to keep my body warmed. Except her light does as well.

Both of us stop, hidden from each other by only a thick crop of trees. There's not much to come between us now. What I want is almost here. Then why is it so hard to step forward? Why can't I bring myself to do more?

She's the first to move, creeping closer. I don't bother. I'm exactly where I want to be. She comes into view, covered with branches and leaves at first, but then nothing is in the way of my sister. She's the same. A few wrinkles have formed around her eyes—whether from smiling or worry, it's difficult to tell. There's a stress and strain around her that wasn't there before, but she carries it well. More than that, there's a glow about her. Not her power shining forth, that I can feel with my own, but something more. Like the glow of happiness.

Though we stay silent, it's exactly perfect. Well, except when I say, "You could join us."

"You know I can't."

"I do know." But I had to try. "We're very happy."

Some of the strain on her face seems to ease at that.

She tenses, like something is coming. I stretch my power out, expecting it to be Tavo or Sosha, but no. It's not a Malryx, it's a Zophas. My cue to leave, but I have what I came for. And now that I saw her, now that I know she's not withering under the weight of turning me, and she knows we're happy, my job feels done.

There's that flicker in me that says the Zophas still calls to me. I can't have it back. I don't want it back. I flash the stolen goods at her. "Expect more of this."

I turn to leave, but a single word stops me. "Marsa."

It's not much, yet so very much. "Kaylyn."

She takes a step toward me. "Marsa, I—" She hangs there, her face growing more agonized by the moment. "Things haven't been the same since you left."

"Not for us, either."

"How are Tavo and Sosha?"

I almost want to tell her about Tavo and me, but it feels too much like bonding, something that will never again be. And Sosha, well… "They're fine. At least as much as they can be after being betrayed and forced out into a world that has nothing to offer them."

That look on her face crunches tighter. She bites her lower lip, like she's trying to keep words from tumbling out. Like maybe my words meant something to her. Like she feels guilty and wants to apologize, but of course, can't.

"I know you are, Kaylyn, and I understand."

She raises her eyebrows at me.

"What?" I ask. "You think we grew up together all those years and I couldn't figure out what you really meant?"

"But if you know...?"

"I didn't when you betrayed me, but after thinking about it, I knew it couldn't be any other way. You would never do something so cruel without cause."

"But you're still Malryx."

"It suits me better than I expected." Everything makes so much more sense on this side of things. "You wouldn't believe what I've learned."

She takes the bait, just like I hoped. "What?"

"Zophas and Malryx are opposites, yes, and you may have light, but it's not good like you think. It's a savage light that forces other to follow under it or be killed."

"No, we help people. We're kind. We've only killed those—"

"Who the Aster and Astra sent you after. Those who opposed them. Those who I'm now like. And all I'm doing, Kaylyn, is trying to survive."

"No, it's not like that. You've hurt people."

"Have I?" I raise an eyebrow at her. "Maybe. But only those who tried to not let me survive. Those who would get in the way of Sosha and Tavo's survival."

"But hurting them? That's not like you."

"Maybe it wasn't before, but now that I've protected others for a while..." I've done what I must.

Suddenly she smiles like I've just given her the best present ever. For the briefest insane moment, I have a crazy hope she's turning, but when I reach out to her with my Malkine, her Zophasken is still gratingly bright.

"I have waited a long time for a worthy opponent," she says.

"You may have trouble keeping up with me." I suppose if we can't be friends like before, we might as well find some other way to spend our time together. And I know her so well; it will only be too easy to play tricks on her.

I say, "Don't worry. I'll keep your little secret about your true intentions from Sosha and Tavo. They're still learning what I already know, and they're so much more effective when they have your betrayal to focus on."

"You always were better at lying than I was."

I sure am. Sometimes lies need to be told in

order to achieve what needs to happen.

There's a crack, like a branch being stepped on. One of her little Zophas friends by the feel of my power. Jorrin, her stolen love. Just because I understand doesn't mean I'm entirely done being hurt by it.

"Lover boy is here," I say.

"We'll meet again soon.

"Sooner than you think."

She grins at me, and then turns away, back toward the trees. I run then, not running away, but saving our game for another day. My purpose is met. Though I hoped she would come with me, I knew it was unlikely, but now she doesn't hold the guilt of turning me.

I meet up with Tavo, and together, we look down on the valley. He puts an arm around me, and we watch the two distant black dots that we can feel powered with light head back toward their little village.

"You could have captured her. Ransomed her or something, at the very least."

As I look out over the valley, I grin. "I know."

The End

If you enjoyed reading this book, please consider helping the author by leaving a review where you purchased the book and/or on Goodreads.

You can sign up to receive notification when Janeal Falor releases a new book at http://eepurl.com/AL2s5 or www.janealfalor.com with a Release Notification link on the side bar, along with links to deleted scenes. Or talk to the author directly at janealfalor@gmail.com

Read Janeal's debut novel, the National Bestselling, YOU ARE MINE

More by Janeal Falor

Mine to Tarnish (Mine #.5)

Katherine's place is the same as any woman's—on the shelf next to the dresses and bolts of cloth. When she's sold to a warlock, life grows even bleaker. Her new owner is as old and rancid as he is cruel, driving her to do the unthinkable: run.

Nothing prepared her for being on her own. And she's definitely unprepared for the warlocks hunting her down. But she must stay one step ahead because if caught, the best she can hope for is death.

You Are Mine (Mine #1)

Serena knows a few simple things. She will always be owned by a warlock. She will never have freedom. She will always do what her warlock wishes, regardless of how inane, frivolous, or cruel it is. And if she doesn't follow the rules, she will be tarnished. Spelled to be bald, inked, and barren for the rest of her life—worth less than the shadow she casts.

Then her ownership is won by a barbarian from another country. With the uncertainty that comes from belonging to a new warlock, Serena questions if being tarnished is really worse than being owned by a barbarian, and tempts fate by breaking the rules. When he looks the other way instead of punishing her, she discovers a new world. The more she ventures into the forbidden, the more she learns of love and a freedom just out of reach. Serena longs for both. But in a society where women are only ever property, hoping for more could be deadly.

Mine to Spell (Mine #2)

Cynthia has always hidden from her father's hexes behind her older sister. When her family gains independence unheard of for women, she's relieved that her days of harsh punishments are over. But as her seventeenth birthday approaches--the typical age to be sold to a new master--death threats endanger her sisters. She now faces two options: run or meet society's expectations.

For once, Cynthia isn't going to let her older sister shield her from the problem. She's going to prove to herself, her sisters, and society that her family isn't a threat to their traditions. She willingly chooses to be purchased by a new master. A bold step that takes her somewhere she never thought she would go and to a man she might possibly fall in love with. With his help, she may just find a way to save her sisters while discovering how to stand up for herself. If she lives long enough.

Acknowledgments

Thank you to so many people who have supported my journey and helped this book become a reality. To Stephanie for pointing out so many details I was missing. Sarah for saving me from swearing out injuries and scared doors among many other things. And a huge thanks for Sotia for putting up with a really crumby first draft.

As always, my family and friends have been a huge support to me, especially as I was working on this book. Rebecca for constantly supporting me and taking the time to have many shakes with me. Karen for letting me chat when I needed to. Mom and Dad for being such amazing parents. I don't think I could have done any better. For Tai, Xandria, and Will for being so loving and patient. Biggest thanks goes to Erik. I can't imagine my life without you. I love you all!

About the Author

Amazon best selling author Janeal Falor lives in Utah with her husband and three children. In her non-writing time she teaches her kids to make silly faces, cooks whatever strikes her fancy, and attempts to cultivate a garden even when half the things she plants die. When it's time for a break she can be found taking a scenic drive with her family or drinking hot chocolate.